He didn't look like an attorney

His dark wavy hair was tidy enough and he wore a well-cut, charcoal suit...but something about his sprawling pose said I-make-my-own-laws-thanks-very-much. And yet he definitely wasn't a client. Megan could tell from the way the other ambulance-chasers were angled toward him. As if he was the chief of some unruly tribe.

Still laughing, relaxed in a way Megan didn't think she'd ever been, he let his gaze wander the room. She didn't bother to glance away—people tended to overlook her. In court her lack of visibility was a secret weapon. With her dad, it was a pain in the butt and a childhood resentment she knew she should have gotten over by now.

To her surprise, the guy didn't look past her for a more out-there woman. He grinned at Megan. Nothing flirtatious, just friendly, one side of his mouth quirking in a way that was...

Delicious.

Dear Reader,

Romance novels have changed a lot since I read my first one at age fourteen. But for me, my favorite elements remain the same and, thankfully, are still going strong. The strong-minded, successful men I've always loved are still around, but now they meet their match in equally, but differently, strong and successful women.

Her Secret Rival is the story of two people who think they know exactly what they want from life and how to get it. But their best-laid plans are disrupted by an attraction that's too powerful to ignore. Because what could be more important than the love of your life... even if you have to overcome more than a few obstacles to attain it?

I do hope you enjoy *Her Secret Rival*. To read a couple of extra After-the-End scenes, visit the For Readers page at www.abbygaines.com.

Sincerely,

Abby Gaines

Her Secret Rival
Abby Gaines

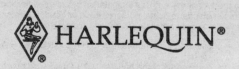

HARLEQUIN®

TORONTO • NEW YORK • LONDON
AMSTERDAM • PARIS • SYDNEY • HAMBURG
STOCKHOLM • ATHENS • TOKYO • MILAN • MADRID
PRAGUE • WARSAW • BUDAPEST • AUCKLAND

Recycling programs for this product may not exist in your area.

ISBN-13: 978-0-373-71597-8

HER SECRET RIVAL

ABOUT THE AUTHOR

Abby Gaines wrote her first romance novel as a teenager. She typed it up and sent it to Mills & Boon in London, who promptly rejected it. A flirtation with a science fiction novel never really got off the ground, so Abby put aside her writing ambitions as she went to college, then began her working life at IBM. When she and her husband had their first baby, Abby worked from home as a freelance business journalist...and soon after that the urge to write romance resurfaced. It was another five long years before Abby sold her first novel to Harlequin Superromance in 2006. She also writes for Harlequin NASCAR.

Abby lives with her husband and children—and a Labradoodle and a cat—in a house with enough stairs to keep her fit and a sun-filled office whose sea view provides inspiration for the funny, tender romances she loves to write. Visit her at www.abbygaines.com.

Books by Abby Gaines

HARLEQUIN SUPERROMANCE
1397—WHOSE LIE IS IT ANYWAY?
1414—MARRIED BY MISTAKE
1480—THE DIAPER DIARIES
1539—THE GROOM CAME BACK
1585—HER SO-CALLED FIANCÉ

HARLEQUIN NASCAR
BACK ON TRACK
FULLY ENGAGED

With love to Sandra Hyatt, who's traveled the peaks and bumps with me for longer than either of us might care to admit.

Thanks for being such great company!

CHAPTER ONE

"YOUR HONOR, WHAT matters most here? A hunk of tin and four wheels, or that three children get to spend Christmas with the mom they love?"

Megan Merritt knew that in describing a Mercedes CLK500 convertible as a hunk of tin, she risked losing the sympathy of Judge Potter, presiding over Courtroom 1-C in Atlanta's Fulton County Superior Court. But she'd weighed that risk and decided the need to keep her client out of jail justified it.

She clasped her hands in front of her so she wouldn't fiddle with the button on her pale gray suit jacket. "When my client was driven to deface her husband's car—" *deface* being a euphemism for *pour paint stripper over* "—she was conscious only that he'd made love with his mistress in that car, while his children waited for a father who never showed up to kiss them good-night." Megan kept her voice low and neutral. Despite the emotional subject, she was presenting facts. Theatrics weren't her style.

Judge Potter pursed his lips, removed his spectacles and polished them with his handkerchief. Megan took that as disapproval of Mrs. Carter's failure to consider the consequences of her actions. This was an incarceration-worthy offence, that deliberate rubbing seemed to say.

Mrs. Carter wouldn't go to prison if Megan had anything to do with it.

She continued her closing argument, making sure to maintain eye contact with the judge, except when a dismissive glance at the husband and his attorney was required.

"And so," Megan concluded, "in light of my client's genuine and justifiable distress, and of the fact that her children have already been abandoned by one parent, I ask the Court to exercise leniency."

The judge thanked her and the opposing counsel and adjourned the case. He would announce his sentence after lunch.

Along with everyone else, Megan stood while he left the courtroom.

"What should I do now?" Brandi Carter asked in her little-girl voice. It was a question she posed often—Megan imagined that, until recently, Brandi had seldom made major decisions. The thought was both appealing and repugnant.

"The judge will be at least an hour," Megan said. "Take a break, I'll call you when you need to come back."

Brandi squeezed Megan's hand. "Thank you." She was a sweet woman who didn't deserve the pain she'd been through.

Megan watched her walk hesitantly out of the near-empty courtroom, alone after years of marriage to a husband she adored. Megan shivered.

Then her gaze alighted on the tall, silver-haired man seated in the back row. He'd come! She'd hoped, of course, that he would read the material she'd sent over this morning, but she'd not really expected… This had to be a good sign. Megan's heart beat faster, and she steadied her hands as she gathered her papers into her briefcase.

By the time she walked briskly down the aisle, she was the collected professional her father needed to see.

"Hi, Dad." She kissed his cheek, and couldn't help beaming at him. *Don't take anything for granted,* she thought.

Jonah Merritt levered himself out of his chair, holding on for just a moment to the seat back in front of him. "I'll buy you a coffee," he said.

She couldn't tell what he was thinking—small wonder, given he'd made a career out of being inscrutable in the courtroom. But he wouldn't be here if it wasn't good news, would he? She had a crazy urge to ask of him what she'd asked of Judge Potter: *leniency.* Maybe that wasn't the right word. She wanted her father to withhold the certainty that made him think he knew her, knew the limit of her abilities. Just this once.

"Let's go next door," Megan said. "I don't want to get across town and have the clerk call to say the judge is back."

They walked out of the courthouse tower on to Central Avenue, where the weak November sunshine battled a bone-deep chill. Almost before she could shiver, they were indoors again, inside The Jury Room, a bar and café frequented by lawyers and, less often, their clients.

Several people hailed Jonah as the two of them made their way to a table in the corner of the L-shaped room. Everyone wanted to know how the founder and senior partner of Merritt, Merritt & Finch, one of Atlanta's most prestigious law firms, was doing after the heart attack that had almost killed him a few months back. Jonah replied with unnecessary evasion—the grapevine had long since established that his health was forcing him to retire. The only mystery was who would take over from him.

By the time they sat down, Megan's nerves were stretched tight, and it was nothing to do with the judgment she was awaiting. She settled herself in her chair, put her cell phone on the table, knowing better than to rush her dad.

"Risky closing back there." Jonah jerked his head in the direction of the courthouse. "You'd better hope Judge Potter doesn't drive a convertible Mercedes."

It was one thing having her courtroom rivals continuously underestimate her...but having her father still do it after twenty-eight years rankled.

Megan spread her fingers on the table, pressing them into the polished wooden surface. "The judge drives a three-year-old Chevrolet sedan. His two cars before that were also Chevrolet sedans. His last two vacations were in the U.S.A." She was counting on the judge having little sympathy toward owners of flashy, foreign sports cars.

Her father chuckled. "I should have known you'd be on top of it."

"You should have," she agreed, suddenly fierce.

Jonah puffed out his cheeks, then said, "Potter will rule for your client, no doubt about it."

Her dad had practiced law in Atlanta for forty-some years, and when he called a verdict, he called it right. If he wasn't certain, he didn't call it.

She liked to think she'd inherited his instincts, his focus. And that he would see that.

To be on the safe side, she ordered an espresso, rather than the Christmas latte with gingerbread syrup and whipped cream. Jonah considered all frothy coffees frivolous—if Megan's younger sister Sabrina had been here, he'd have ordered her the fanciest latte in the place, with an indulgent smile.

Megan modeled herself on her older sister, Cynthia, though she couldn't bring herself to order the double-shot Cynthia would have.

She knew Jonah would like a double-shot—he and Cynthia were kindred spirits—but he was on decaf thanks to a couple of postoperative complications. He muttered "decaf" to the server so quietly, it was plain he was hoping the guy wouldn't hear. When his coffee arrived, he took one sip and grimaced—obviously there was nothing wrong with the server's ears.

"Tell me what's going on with the O'Shea case." Jonah needed Megan to keep him informed, thanks to his cardiologist's decree that the office was forbidden territory. In the past, he'd have asked Cynthia, but Cyn had been on a break from the firm, gaining prosecution experience as a district attorney. In the past twelve months Megan and her dad had talked more than they had in twenty-eight years.

Now, she had an opportunity to make the new bond between her and her dad permanent. If only they would move on to the reason Dad was here....

"The O'Shea team is ready to go to court next week." She filled her father in on the details of the complex homicide defense the firm was handling. Megan wasn't working on the case; she was the partner in charge of the family law division of Merritt, Merritt & Finch. "I know the team plans to emphasize that the brother had more motive than O'Shea," she said, "but I think they need to pull a few more people into the net if they're going to challenge reasonable doubt."

Her father nodded once. "Good."

Was this a test?

Suddenly afraid to know, Megan let herself be distracted by a burst of laughter, rising over the piped Christmas carols. She glanced across the room. No surprises, the hilarity came from what her colleagues called Ambulance Corner. The lawyers who frequented the far corner, next to the crowded but untouched magazine rack, were more likely to be drinking beer than coffee. And if they weren't exactly ambulance chasers, they took the cases that were too low-rent or too far-fetched or just too plain unimportant for firms like Merritt, Merritt & Finch.

The Ambulance Corner crowd were all men, most of them vaguely familiar. But the booming laugh that had caught Megan's notice belonged to a man she hadn't seen before. He'd captured the attention of most of the other women in the room, too.

Maybe because he didn't look like an attorney. His dark wavy hair was tidy enough and he wore a well-cut charcoal suit…but something about his sprawling pose said I-make-my-own-laws-thanks-very-much. And yet, he definitely wasn't a client. Megan could tell from the way the other ambulance guys were angled toward him. As if he were the chief.

Still laughing, relaxed in a way Megan didn't think she'd ever been, the Chief let his gaze wander the room. She didn't bother to glance away—people tended to overlook her. In court, her invisibility was a secret weapon. With her dad, it was a pain in the butt and a childhood resentment she knew she should have gotten over by now.

To her surprise, the Chief didn't look past her for a more out-there woman. He grinned at Megan. Nothing flirtatious, just friendly, one side of his mouth quirking in a way that was...

Delicious.

Excuse me? Where had that come from?

Megan felt the color crawling up her face. Chief-guy grinned wider, then he leaned into the guy next to him and said something. The other man, who wore a dark green suit when no one from a reputable firm wore anything but gray or black, eyed Megan.

The Chief was asking who she was! Megan looked determinedly away, back at her father. She picked up her cup, took a sip of the too-bitter brew. She imagined the green suit telling the Chief her name, imagined the recognition, imagined him looking at her with...

What? Disappointment that she was out of his league?

Yeah, that happened to her all the time. Carefully, she pressed her palms to her cheeks. She chanced a glance back at the Chief.

He was talking seriously now to someone across the table. Quite clearly, he wasn't the victim of a sudden heat wave.

"So," her father said, "what do you think?"

She stared at him, aghast. What had she missed?

Jonah chuckled. "Don't fret, sweetie, I know what it's like when you're waiting for a judge to make up his mind. But I told you, this one's in the bag."

"I can't help worrying," she murmured, seizing the excuse. "Brandi doesn't deserve to go to jail."

Her father shook his head. "You're just like Cynthia, can't leave your work in the office."

I'm just like me, Megan wanted to say.

"I worry that you work too hard," Jonah said.

"I like my work. I love it."

"Which brings me," he continued, "to the reason for this meeting."

At last.

He reached into the inside pocket of his jacket, and pulled out the material she'd sent him—her résumé and a letter detailing why she thought she should take over as head of Merritt, Meritt & Finch after Jonah formally retired. "You should have brought this to me in person," he said.

"I wanted you to take an objective look at my skills," she replied. Because on paper, she was better qualified than anyone to run the firm. Whereas face-to-face, she was always the daughter who wasn't as smart as Cynthia, and who wasn't as beautiful and charming as Sabrina.

"Truth is, I've never thought of you as a candidate for head of the firm," Jonah said with characteristic honesty.

Sometimes, Megan thought, honesty was overrated. "That's because you—we *all*—assumed Cynthia would take over." Nowadays, the speculation was that Cynthia had a brilliant career ahead of her as a judge. Some had even mentioned the Georgia Supreme Court in the distant future.

"You need someone who loves the firm as much as you do," Megan said. "That's me. You need someone with excellent legal qualifications—I graduated magna cum laude from Harvard. You need someone who can help grow the business—I built our family law division from scratch, and it's been profitable almost from day one."

"It represents just twenty percent of our revenue," he reminded her.

"Which is why I've made a point of understanding the other divisions," she said. The commercial and criminal practices each represented about forty percent of the firm's turnover. "I'm confident I can help bring in clients across the board."

"It's not just about your capabilities," Jonah said. "I need someone who commands the respect of all the partners."

"Name one partner who doesn't respect me."

"You keep such a low profile outside your practice, they don't know you," Jonah said. "How can they respect you? Megan—" he pushed his cup away, the decaffeinated sludge untouched "—I love you, you're my daughter, you're an excellent lawyer. But you're not the kind of person I have in mind to lead the firm."

How could she be, when she was never in his mind at all?

"I'll admit I'm a quiet achiever." She used the phrase that had appeared in every school report she'd ever brought home. "I'm not as outgoing as you and Cynthia. But there's more than one way to do this job."

"I'm not convinced you can attract the big clients we need in commercial, and that's where the growth is. I'm not convinced I can sell you to the other partners as their new boss." He began checking off his points on his fingers, "I'm not convinced you have the handle on the business that Cynthia does." He stopped, three fingers in the air, three top-notch reasons for him to overlook her once again.

"I'm sorry, Megan," he said, "you're not a candidate."

Her cell phone rang, and through a haze of tears that she would never, in a million years, let her dad see, Megan recognized it was the courthouse. She answered, listened to the clerk. "Thanks, I'll be right there."

She pushed her chair away from the table. "Potter's back." Already she was stabbing Brandi's number into her phone, her finger thankfully steady.

"I won't come with you." Jonah stood. "I know you've won."

Megan negotiated her way past clusters of dark-suited lawyers engrossed in conversations, doubtless unaware of her existence. Then past Ambulance Corner—she was no longer interested to know whether the Chief was noticing her departure. Failure beat a tattoo at her temples, drumming up a headache that somehow had a matching pain in her heart. Her father's confidence in her imminent victory for Brandi Carter did nothing to console her.

What does it matter if I win the battle, if I've already lost the war?

CHAPTER TWO

BRANDI CARTER WAS sentenced to thirty hours' community service, which she could complete at her son's preschool.

"You're a genius," she said to Megan.

"Tell that to my dad," Megan muttered.

Back in the office, she left the Carter file for Trisha, her paralegal, to wrap up, and summoned a list of pending cases to her screen. She was too ticked off to concentrate on a new case, so she might as well start allocating associates to clients.

After that, she moved on to monitoring the family practice's finances—still billing more hours per head, and thus making more profit, than the other divisions. If Dad would let her at the rest of the business, she could bring clients in, she knew it.

The trouble with admin was that once you started, it ate up the time. Megan forced herself to stop at eight o'clock—the partners' floor was nearly deserted. As she switched off her PC, her direct line rang.

"Got a lead for you." The raspy voice could only belong to Bill Chain, a private investigator she occasionally hired for the kind of detective work needed in divorce cases.

"Hello to you, too, Bill."

He made a chuffing sound. "You want the name?"

"Yes, please." She picked up a pen.

The detective paused. "Theo Hoskins."

Megan dropped the pen. "Are you sure?" Theo Hoskins and his wife, Barbara, were one of Atlanta's wealthiest, most prominent—and reputedly happiest—couples.

"I delivered him some photos tonight. One peek and he was asking for a recommendation on a lawyer."

People often didn't want to use their regular family lawyer for a divorce.

"He wanted three names," Chain said. "Yours was one of the ones I gave him."

Megan's mind whirred as she finished the call. Theo Hoskins was a well-known philanthropist and property developer. They called him the Trump of the South, as much for his flair for self-publicity as for his wealth. She wanted to handle his divorce, of course. But what if this time, she went after more? Theo's extensive business interests made him one of the most sought-after commercial clients in Atlanta. He used a couple of large law firms...but not Merritt, Merritt & Finch.

She'd had high-profile divorce clients before, but hadn't pursued other opportunities with them. It hadn't felt right to take advantage of someone's personal distress.

Right now, her own personal distress was at record levels, and it sure didn't feel right that her father wouldn't even consider her to head the firm.

If Megan could convince Theo Hoskins to hire her to represent him in the divorce...and if she impressed him with her work...and if she convinced him to transfer his commercial business to Merritt, Merritt & Finch...

Okay, so that was a lot of ifs. But they were all achievable. Not only would she boost the family division's profile and prove its value to the rest of the firm, but she'd have made a significant contribution to her dad's precious commercial practice. A contribution no one could overlook.

MEGAN STAYED in the office until the small hours, unearthing every available scrap of information about Theo and Barbara Hoskins, and sorting them by relevance.

When she was satisfied she knew everything she could be expected to, and several things she couldn't, she crashed for a few hours at her apartment. At seven, she started making calls. She had to find the cheated-on husband before the other two lawyers the detective had recommended got to him.

It took tenacity, the rescheduling of several appointments, and a flight to Dallas on Theo Hoskins's private jet, but by seven that evening, Megan had a new client.

The flight turned out to be the only time Theo had available to talk. Impressed by her efforts to track him down, he'd invited her along for the ride. After they landed, he went to a meeting, and Megan boarded a commercial flight back to Atlanta. All the way home, she'd itched to use the seat-back phone to call her father with the good news, but client confidentiality made that impossible.

When they landed it was too late to phone Jonah. Instead, she waited until the earliest possible hour the next morning that she could call without startling her dad into another heart attack.

"The Hoskinses are getting divorced?" Jonah's voice rose.

"Theo says Barbara plans to take him to the cleaners." Megan poured granola into a bowl and upended a carton of yogurt over it. Her client was naturally reluctant to let his wife walk off with hundreds of millions of dollars. "Of course, Barbara's successful in her own right, so disentangling their entitlements could be complicated."

"This is big," Jonah said. "The press will be all over it, just like with Paul McCartney and that woman."

It wasn't quite in the same league, but her dad had a point. "We'll be as discreet as we can, but yeah, it's a headline case." Megan held the phone closer to her ear, and stirred the granola into the yogurt. "When this is over," she said casually, "I plan to ask Theo to give Merritt, Merritt & Finch some of his commercial work." Stating her objective aloud sent a surge of excitement through her.

"I see." Her father sounded surprised, in a good way. Then he added, "But first, you need to focus on the divorce. If Theo doesn't come out of that feeling as if he's won, you won't stand a chance with anything else."

As if she didn't know that.

"I suppose Barbara's hired some hotshot Manhattan lawyer," he continued. Mrs. Hoskins was from New York.

"I don't know," Megan admitted. At her father's disapproving silence she added, "Yet."

To her frustration, she felt the ground she'd gained when she'd signed Theo slipping away.

"I plan to win this case, then win Theo Hoskins's commercial business," she said firmly. And refused to take her father's silence as doubt.

Her dad now fully in the loop, Megan ate her breakfast, the silence of her apartment broken only by the crunch of granola. This was her favorite thinking time.

Whoever Barbara Hoskins hired would make a big difference to how easy Megan's job was. If it was any of the regular Atlanta crowd, she was sure she could win.

But if it was, as Dad said, a hotshot New Yorker... *I can still beat them. I just need to know my enemy.*

FOR SOME INCOMPREHENSIBLE reason, Barbara Hoskins chose not to appoint a lawyer from the top echelons of the profession in Atlanta or even New York. Megan's admin assistant took a call from the assistant of one Travis Jamieson of Prescott Palmer Associates. Mr. Jamieson was representing Mrs. Hoskins and had requested a meeting with Megan to scope out the case. When the assistants couldn't find a time during the day, Mr. Jamieson's assistant suggested dinner. Megan's assistant agreed.

When the appointment notice popped up in Megan's e-mail, she gave a whoop of excitement that had Trisha, her paralegal, swiveling in her chair at the meeting table in Megan's office, where they'd been running through a stack of depositions.

"Barbara Hoskins is represented by Prescott Palmer," Megan announced.

Trisha took off her reading glasses. "Is that a joke?"

Megan read the e-mail again. "I don't know Travis Jamieson, but if he's a divorce lawyer at PPA, how good can he be?"

"Bad." Trisha ran a hand through her graying curls. "Or very bad."

Prescott Palmer had a halfway decent property division, but most of its business was family law, and the more dysfunctional the family the better. When sleaze made headlines in a divorce case, the odds were PPA was representing one of the parties. The firm's strength lay in its ability to force a trial by media rather than in the courtroom.

Surely Mrs. Hoskins wouldn't want her most intimate details dragged through the press?

Megan squinted at her screen, as if the answer to the mystery might lie there. "His assistant made a reservation at Salt." One of Atlanta's finest restaurants.

"Trying to impress you," Trisha suggested. She sniggered.

"Meaning what?" Megan asked.

"Meaning you're almost as hard to impress as your father and your sister."

Megan threw a balled-up piece of paper at her. "I am not."

Trisha put her glasses back on. "Whatever you say." She filed away the deposition she'd just transcribed. "But if Travis Jamieson didn't work for PPA, I'd feel sorry for the guy. He won't know what's hit him."

MEGAN ARRIVED at Salt ten minutes early, with the intention of putting Travis Jamieson at a disadvantage by forcing him to apologize for keeping her waiting.

"Your dinner companion is already seated," the maître d' told her as he helped her out of the coat she wore over her rust-colored silk jersey wrap dress.

So much for catching him unawares. It was Megan who was forced to quickly gather her thoughts as she followed the maître d' across the restaurant. He stopped at a table in the center of the room. "Ms. Merritt has arrived, sir."

A dark-haired man stood and turned to face her.

Megan blinked, curling her fingers at her sides so she wouldn't rub her eyes like a bemused moron. This was no stranger. This was the "Chief" from The Jury Room. *What's going on?*

"Megan, nice to meet you. I'm Travis Jamieson." He stuck out his hand and smiled at her. His mouth was generous, and his charcoal-dark eyes gleamed as he scanned her face and figure. Slowly, not so much assessing as...noticing.

"Pleased to meet you, too." She shook that strong hand, making her clasp as firm as she could. But where her strength was calculated, his was careless, relaxed.

She slid into the seat across the table from him. The waiter poured her a glass of Chardonnay from a bottle Travis had evidently ordered without waiting to learn her preference. She used the small lull to reassert her lawyer's brain. So Travis Jamieson was possessed of a certain primal male appeal, so what? He was still somewhere near the bottom of Atlanta's legal hierarchy, and she could take him in a court battle anytime.

She colored at the thought of taking him. What was wrong with her? Was she that starved for attention that one long look from a pair of dark eyes had her fantasizing?

"I saw you last week in The Jury Room," she said. It would be stupid to pretend she hadn't. "You asked someone who I was."

He shook his head. "I knew who you were." His gravelly voice set up a tingle between her shoulder blades.

Really? "Quite a coincidence that I should see you for the first time last week, then end up opposing you on a case."

"Good lawyers know there's no such thing as coincidence," he said. There was a small but unmistakable emphasis on the "good," and a teasing inflection in his voice that she decided not to respond to.

"Exactly my point," she said crisply. "What's going on?"

He picked up his menu. "Sometimes, good lawyers are wrong. I didn't know last week that I would be representing Barbara Hoskins…that you would be representing Theo."

As she scanned her own menu, Megan wondered if he'd at least known of the Hoskinses' plans to divorce. Even more, she wondered how Barbara had come to appoint him. But like many lawyers, she preferred not to ask questions to which she didn't know the answer.

"I represented Barbara's sister in her divorce some years ago," Travis said. "Barbara felt her sister came out of it with more than they expected. I guess that gave her the confidence to hire me."

Megan blinked. He'd just answered her unspoken question, no games, no tricks. "I'm not sure I remember…"

He grinned, obviously knowing she planned to look it up. "Mallory versus Mallory, Augusta Superior Court."

She'd never heard of it, thank goodness. Travis Jamieson couldn't have handled a divorce this high profile before. She hadn't either, but she'd come close, and she knew the demands this kind of case put on an attorney. Even if Travis aimed to play it straight, with any luck, he'd be exhausted in a week. She and her client would steamroller through to victory.

She wasn't about to warn him of the scale of the

challenge. Why scare him into trying harder? The secret to her success was that other lawyers barely noticed her, and that made them overconfident.

Although Travis, it seemed, *had* noticed her. She could only assume he was one of those men who eyed up any woman, just for the sake of it.

"How long have you worked at Prescott Palmer Associates?" She chose the dull sort of question he could answer on autopilot, so that those intense dark eyes would move away from her face.

It worked. He leaned back, reached for a bread roll from the basket in the center of the table. "I had a few years with a big firm in Dallas after I got my degree, then came back to Atlanta ten years ago to join Prescott Palmer. Kyle Prescott and I were in college together." He broke open the roll, began buttering it.

Megan fought the downturn of her lips. Prescott was reportedly a graduate of Dayton University in Ohio. Rumor had it he'd been thrown out of an East Coast school in his first year for cheating and Dayton was the only place that would take him. If it was true you could judge a man by the company he kept, then Travis Jamieson was…not exactly shady, but a small step above it. Prescott Palmer Associates milked mediocre cases to an extent that made other lawyers shake their heads.

But she wasn't about to criticize opposing counsel. She would assume Travis was, like her, a professional who could discuss the merits of his client's case objectively. Even if he worked for a bunch of cowboys.

Right now, he looked so laid-back, arms loosely at his sides, head thrown back, she could imagine he had a horse tethered outside and a range to ride. *That wasn't the kind of cowboy I meant.*

And when had "know her enemy" expanded to include the color of his eyes, or the way his chin dimpled when he smiled?

Was he flirting with her in some subliminal way that she didn't understand? It was more than possible, she conceded.

The waiter took their orders, and Megan sipped her wine as she cast about for a topic that wouldn't put her in mind of popular romantic fantasies, but which wouldn't encourage Travis to take her seriously as an opponent. If he'd done any research, he would know she won most of her cases. But lawyers were an arrogant breed; it didn't take much for them to discount the evidence and assume it was others' incompetence, rather than her skills, that had prevailed.

TRAVIS BUTTERED another roll while he watched Megan out of the corner of his eye; it seemed to disconcert her when he looked directly at her. He could practically see the cogs turning. He'd heard she was supersmart, and it hadn't taken her half a second to figure out there was a link between his presence in The Jury Room last week and tonight's dinner. Even if, at the time, he'd had no idea this dinner would happen.

Last week, she'd worn a gray suit that was all business, and it was her stillness that had drawn Travis's attention from the more familiar figure of her father. When she'd left the café, she'd seemed on the verge of tears. Worried about her case? Later, Travis heard she'd scored a great result in a sentencing hearing—her nutcase client who practically destroyed an eighty-thousand-dollar car had got community service. Which reinforced what he knew: Megan Merritt was a first-rate lawyer.

He couldn't think why he hadn't noticed her before. She wasn't exactly pretty, although she had a nicely shaped face and big eyes. In the dress she wore today, made out of some kind of clinging fabric, it was clear she had an alluring figure to go with her admirable brain. Definitely worth watching.

Travis could only put her previous invisibility down to her air of restraint, an aloofness that erected a barrier between her and others. Which he should *not* find intriguing, given that she reminded him of the women he'd met in college. Women who thought a blue-collar guy was good for a fling but not someone to take seriously, in class or in life.

He'd seen her reaction to his mention of Kyle Prescott, and it was pretty clear she judged Travis guilty by association. That was fine—best for her to believe he was her inferior in the courtroom.

He leaned back. "So, you handle many divorces?" Which was like asking Venus Williams if she played much tennis.

Megan sat back, too, and the movement highlighted her curvy figure. "Some," she said demurely, her eyes wide. "How about you?"

"Commercial's more my thing," he said truthfully. "My last divorce was Barbara's sister's." He paused, then said, "Not that it was *my* divorce. I've never been married."

He eyed her bare ring finger. Her glance skittered away and she raised her water glass to her mouth, concentrated on taking a long, slow sip. She was definitely uncomfortable with any man-woman interaction between them.

"But I'd like to be," he said thoughtfully.

Megan sputtered on her water. "Excuse me?"

"I'd like to get married," he said. "You know, start a family."

Her face reddened. "If that's your idea of a pickup line…"

He held up his hands and grinned. "I just got a little sidetracked."

She looked irritated, not like someone who was worried he might be good enough to beat her in court.

He pushed a little further. "Are you married?"

"Could we be professional about this?" she demanded.

"That wasn't a line, either. It's relevant to the Hoskins case."

"How?" she asked.

"I'm trying to figure out your attitude to divorce, because it'll influence your client."

She looked at him as if that was the stupidest thing she'd ever heard. She opened her mouth, then she closed it again. "I'm not married."

He fixed his gaze on her brown eyes. They were unexpectedly warm. "Y'know, that surprises me. You being so pretty."

He felt a twinge of guilt at employing Prescott Palmer style tactics on her. But no doubt Merritt, Merritt & Finch had its own little tricks to unnerve opposing counsel. When it came to protecting a client's interests, all was fair.

Megan wasn't sure if she should slap Travis's face or slap him with a sexual harassment suit.

Neither. If she vented her true thoughts, she wouldn't be able to stop herself from giving him a dressing-down that would warn him of her capabilities in a courtroom.

But how to respond? The few men who'd told her she was pretty were Ivy Leaguers, lawyers whose names were almost as well-known as Merritt. Nice guys, smart guys. *Dull guys.* She had no idea how to handle a man like Travis.

She drew from the same well of desperation that had led her to chase Theo Hoskins halfway across the country, and said sweetly, "And you're a pretty man."

He roared with laughter, turning heads in the hush of the restaurant.

"That's the first time a woman's told me I'm pretty," he said.

She didn't want him laughing at her, she wanted him unsettled, the way she was. She leaned forward. "Y'know, that surprises me." She parroted his earlier words. "You have deep, dark eyes, the longest lashes, a well-shaped mouth…" She'd gone too far, *way* too far for her own peace of mind.

He leaned forward, too, so that well-shaped mouth was very close. "That's interesting, because your lips are rather appealing, as well."

The charge of electricity that snapped between them was almost physical.

Megan shot backward in her seat. "Okay, whatever this game is, you're better at it than I am." She hated that she sounded breathless.

Travis straightened lazily. "I'm not so sure about that."

The waiter delivered their entrées, bringing the game to a merciful end.

"How about we talk about the Hoskinses?" Travis picked up his knife and fork. "My client is prepared to be reasonable."

"So is mine. I assume Mrs. Hoskins doesn't plan to fight the grounds for divorce?"

"They're her grounds, why would she?" Travis looked puzzled. "Habitual intoxication is automatic grounds for divorce in the Georgia code."

Megan found herself sputtering again. She put down her glass—it might be safer not to drink in Travis's presence. "Habitual intoxication? *Theo?*"

"That's what Barbara told me." He raised his eyebrows. "Not where you're coming from?"

"Adultery," she said flatly.

Travis swore.

"According to Theo, she had an affair," Megan said.

"She says he gets drunk every night. Maybe he's hallucinating."

"We have photos." Megan's lips pursed in disapproval.

Travis had been having trouble keeping his eyes off those lips ever since they'd turned into a topic of conversation. She'd taken him unawares with her flirting in response to his, but she obviously hadn't meant a word of it. Travis grinned as he absorbed the blow to his ego.

And saw her eyes follow the movement of his mouth. *Fascinating.*

"The question is whether the adultery is what caused the marriage to break down," he said. "Barbara says Theo is drunk nine nights out of ten. That might drive any wife to adultery."

"She has kids, for Pete's sake."

"Irrelevant."

"I don't agree."

Was Megan taking her client's side because it was her job, or was that light in her eyes a spark of anger?

He idled his fork. "I hope you don't plan to let this case turn sleazy."

He almost laughed at her outraged expression.

"Only one of us is likely to turn this case sleazy, Mr. Jamieson—" so, they were on last-name terms now, were they? "—and we both know it's not I." Her voice dripped ice. "Neither of our clients will want to fight this case in the tabloid headlines, so I suggest you rein in whatever mudslinging you plan."

"I plan on winning this fair and square," he assured her. "No dirty tricks."

She tilted her head to one side, as if it hadn't occurred to her he might think he had a chance of winning.

Her reaction wasn't unjustified. Travis had had to go a long way back to find a blot on her court record. And she'd never emerged the loser in a big divorce.

But everyone lost sometimes.

"I'll hold you to your no-dirty-tricks promise," she said.

Through the rest of the meal, they talked process— what information had to be disclosed on each side, whether there was any chance the case wouldn't go to court. Which seemed unlikely. Plus where and when they should hold a meeting with both clients.

The mundane aspects of the conversation were interspersed with the occasional personal comment from Travis, usually leading to a calm put-down from Megan. When they stood to leave, Travis realized he hadn't had such an enjoyable evening in a long time. He almost wished he could take advantage of the mistletoe the restaurant had pinned above the doorway.

"Who's paying for dinner?" Megan asked as she shrugged into her coat. "Your client or mine?"

"Mine," he said. "It's only fair, given yours will be paying later."

The look she gave him as they walked out to the parking lot was definitely not intimidated. Travis escorted her to her car, a sporty red BMW at odds with her reserve. He'd bet she had this car totally under control.

"Thank you for dinner." She stuck out a hand.

He shook it, found himself holding on. Her fingers were cool and steady, just like the rest of her. On impulse, he leaned forward to kiss her cheek. She saw him coming and dodged. But she made the wrong call, went the wrong direction, and his lips brushed across her mouth.

Her mistake was no hardship. Megan's lips were warm and soft, and out of instinct she puckered in response to his kiss. That fleeting half second set Travis afire from head to toe. He jerked his head away.

She touched her mouth, wide-eyed.

"Sorry," he said. "I was going for the cheek."

"Don't go for anything," she ordered. "I'm not in the habit of kissing opposing counsel."

Pity.

He saluted her. "Yes, ma'am."

As he drove his Chevy truck toward his home in one of the few streets in Virginia Highlands that hadn't yet been gentrified, he couldn't shake that kiss. He should have done the damn thing properly, save him thinking about it now.

But he wasn't likely to get the chance. Sooner or later—probably sooner—Megan would discover his true motivation for pestering Barbara Hoskins to let him represent her. And when that happened, kissing him would be the last thing on Megan's mind.

CHAPTER THREE

THE ONE GOOD THING about the dinner she'd shared with Travis Jamieson on Friday night was that Megan was convinced she could win the Hoskins divorce.

Travis might have been...unsettling personally, but professionally she had his number. He'd said nothing of substance when they'd talked about the case. Megan had never been beaten by a graduate of a small Midwestern college. Not by a lawyer who'd flirted with her, either.

Which made her feel marginally better about the embarrassing end to dinner, she told herself on Tuesday, as she reviewed her notes for this morning's meeting.

She'd kissed Travis! The only small mercy was that he'd realized she was trying to duck away and, thankfully, he'd been gentleman enough not to accuse her of actively seeking the kiss.

It was crazy she could still remember the firm warmth of his mouth, the smell of expensive aftershave overlaid with soap and coffee and man.

Megan cleared her mind of anything personal as she pushed open the door of the third-floor conference room. She smiled a greeting at Theo Hoskins and at Trisha, who would take notes on the meeting, and Mark, the junior associate helping her with the case.

"Are you okay?" she asked Theo.

He nodded. She'd met with him alone yesterday, and he'd been outraged about his wife's accusation of habitual drunkenness. If the allegation made it into the newspapers, it would have a serious impact on his business. Megan had spent two hours calming him down so he could take the moral high ground today. Their first step was to paint Barbara Hoskins as the guilty party.

The phone on the table rang, and Trisha answered it. Travis and his client were there. "Send them in," Trisha said.

"Barbara, how are you?" Megan shook Mrs. Hoskins's hand. She'd met the woman several times at charity benefits. Megan judged her to be in her early forties, probably a few years younger than Theo. Like Theo, she was impeccably groomed, and her demeanor was arctic. Which was easier to work with than hysterical, although it was too soon to say whether today's meeting would go that way. You could never tell with divorces.

Megan shook Travis's hand, ignoring the way his eyes drifted to her lips. His custom-made dark suit made him look like a...*I am not even going to* think *foreign prince*.

Trisha phoned coffee orders to a secretary. Travis chose a latte. He could afford to, Megan thought bitterly. He didn't have a serious reputation to maintain.

"Espresso for you, Megan?" Trisha said.

Megan nodded. "Thank you for coming in this morning." She addressed Travis and Barbara, subtly pointing out they were on Merritt, Merritt & Finch's turf. "The purpose of today's meeting is to find areas of common ground before we appear in front of a judge. The more we can agree in the privacy of this room, the less time you spend airing the details of your marriage in a public court."

Both clients nodded. Megan glanced at her notes.

"We need to talk about the grounds for divorce," Travis said. Megan's head shot up. She was leading this meeting, by implication if not by agreement. "We also hope to make a start on financial settlements and custody issues."

Okay, Mr. Hotshot, so you know how a divorce case works. Big deal.

"Thank you, Travis," she said.

His mouth twitched.

"The easiest way to get a low-profile divorce is to claim the marriage is irretrievably broken," Megan said. "But that means both of you will have to drop your current grounds." She could never understand why couples argued over the grounds for divorce. But so often, people wanted to have the final word.

Didn't they know divorce hurt just as much either way?

"You mean, pretend she never cheated on me?" Theo glared at his wife. Megan felt unreasonably annoyed that her client should be the first to crack.

Her annoyance faded a second later when Barbara weighed in with a diatribe about a father whose kids said he "smelled funny" on the rare occasions he turned up in time to read a bedtime story. Then both clients were shouting to be heard over each other, fists clenched on the tabletop.

Travis slammed a hand down on the table, to Megan's irritation, mainly because it startled her as badly as it did everyone else. "If you want to end up on the front page of the *Journal-Constitution*," he said, "you're going the right way about it. Let me give you an idea of what you're facing." He drew on his apparently considerable knowledge of sleazy divorces to paint a horrifying picture of the Hoskins family being dragged through the muck.

"I think we're all agreed we don't want to go there?" Travis glanced around the table, securing nods from both Hoskinses.

"One other thing," Megan said. "The judge is more likely to respect your wishes if it's clear you've made an attempt to save the marriage."

That led to another round of accusations, not as heated as the last. Travis held up a hand. "Megan's right."

She sent him a look that she hoped said, *I know.*

"You two need to attend at least a couple of counseling sessions. If you don't, there's every chance the judge will order it anyway." Judges were increasingly using their powers to force couples to at least attempt reconciliation.

"Make it family counseling," Megan said. "The children should be involved, too. I'll give you the names of a couple of counselors recommended by the Court." She drew a breath and waded into the next battle. "If we can reach agreement on custody of the children, this case will be over much faster."

"I want full custody," Barbara said.

Theo just about blew a gasket. "No way do you get to take my kids. We'll share custody, or I'll have them."

"My client believes their father's alcohol dependency is detrimental to the children's well-being," Travis said to Megan.

"I am not dependent on alcohol," Theo roared. "If you were married to her, you'd need a drink before you could go home at nights, too."

Megan ignored him. "The Court frowns on absent fathers and is likely to welcome our request for joint custody," she told Travis.

"Not where substance addiction is involved," he said. "You might want to look at Smith versus Barrett. Or Larson versus Van Arden." He added helpfully, "Decatur County Court and Clayton County Court."

Okay, so he knew how to research. Megan did, too. She countered with a couple of strong cases of her own, illustrating how women who had affairs could lose their children.

It might have worked, if Travis hadn't cited a case where a woman who'd committed serial adultery had managed to obtain sole custody of her kids from their hardworking, morally upright dad.

To her vexation, Megan ran out of cases to quote. "I don't believe we'll reach agreement on custody today," she said. "I suggest we move on to the matrimonial property." Surely *things* would prove less emotional than children.

In short order, the couple agreed Theo would keep the condo in Dallas and the beach house on the South Carolina coast. He'd already moved out of the family home in Buckhead, here in Atlanta, which Barbara would have. Cars, a boat, artworks, jewelry and furnishings were all dealt with easily.

Then Megan reached item number eighty-four on the list Theo had supplied. "Two Atlanta Hawks executive club seat season passes," she read out loud. "Valued at three thousand dollars apiece."

Travis snorted.

"Excuse me?" she said.

"My husband knows damn well those seats are worth a lot more than that," Barbara objected.

Megan looked at her client.

"I paid three thousand dollars apiece," he said stubbornly.

"They're some of the best seats at the arena," Travis clarified. "A lot of people want them."

"I'm not giving up my ticket," Barbara told her husband. "I was a Hawks fan long before you were. You never even used to like basketball."

"I'm not giving up mine, either," he said. "Not tonight, not any night."

Megan vaguely remembered newspaper headlines about a series of games this week.

"You can't go tonight," Barbara protested. "*I'm* going and I'm not going to sit with you."

Just like that, they were arguing again. Houses and boats might not be emotional, but basketball tickets apparently were.

Two of Megan's colleagues walking past the glass-walled meeting room glanced in. It would be just her luck for someone to call her dad and say she'd lost control of a meeting. With her most important client.

She slammed her hand down on the table, the way Travis had earlier. He was the only one who didn't start.

"Neither of you is going to that game tonight," she said. Travis folded his arms and eyed her with what might have been enjoyment.

Theo's jaw dropped. "But we're playing the Pistons, it's our big chance to get out of this slump."

"You're not going," Megan reiterated. "We can't risk both of you turning up and this becoming a public argument."

"Travis," Barbara said suddenly, "I'd like you to have my ticket."

"That may not be appropriate," Megan began.

"Thanks, Barbara." Travis grinned.

"You can't go with my lawyer," Barbara told her husband triumphantly.

"You might as well take my ticket," Theo grumbled to Megan.

"Thank you," Megan said automatically, "but—"

"Much appreciated, both of you," Travis said smoothly. The look he gave Megan said, *Let's set a good example here.* She subsided with a glare.

Megan checked her watch—four o'clock. It felt as if they'd been here a week. "I suggest we finish for today. You both have a lot to think about. How about we reconvene Thursday?"

Thursday was agreed, and the clients left.

Travis shook hands with Mark and Trisha, then turned to Megan. "What time shall I pick you up for the game?"

It took her a moment to get it. She laughed. "I'm not going."

"Why not? We'll only have to meet again tomorrow to talk through this stuff."

"It's not professional," she said, conscious of how unprofessional things had ended up the other night.

"You had dinner with me." His low tone said, *You kissed me back.*

"It was a dinner *meeting.*"

"This would be a basketball meeting."

"No."

"They're great seats," he coaxed.

"No."

"I'll buy the hot dogs."

"You'll be eating them on your own." Aware of Trisha watching the exchange with interest, Megan held the door open for him to leave.

MEGAN PARKED her BMW in the broad sweep of the driveway outside her father's front door, alongside Cynthia's Volvo and Sabrina's convertible VW Beetle.

She forced herself not to hurry, not to worry about the fact she was last to arrive. Dinner with her dad wasn't a competition, so it was stupid to feel, every time she got together with her family, that she had something to prove.

She found her sisters in the farmhouse-style kitchen, out of place in a house that had never been a farmhouse but welcoming nonetheless.

"Megan, it's so good to see you." Sabrina rushed to hug her as if it had been months, rather than a week, since their last dinner.

"Why, are you looking for a lawyer to write you a prenup?" Megan joked.

There was no way Sabrina would sign a prenup. She and Jake, her fiancé, were so nuts about each other, not even the most jaded attorney—or sister—would seriously suggest it.

She hugged Sabrina back, then crossed the kitchen to kiss Cynthia on the cheek. Cynthia responded, but she seemed distracted.

"I'm making gin fizzes." Sabrina indicated bottles of gin and club soda, plus a pile of limes, on the counter.

Megan realized she was very much in need of a drink. "Light on the fizz, heavy on the gin for me."

Sabrina's wide smile reminded her of all the photos she'd seen of her sister in newspapers and magazines during her recent stint as Miss Georgia. Sabrina had inherited her pale gold hair and sparkling blue eyes from her mom, Jonah's late, beloved second wife.

Megan sniffed at the wonderful aromas coming from the oven. "Dinner smells great. I'm guessing Dad didn't cook."

"Miss Perfect strikes again," Cynthia said, with uncharacteristic irritation.

Megan knew what her older sister meant. Sabrina was not only beauty-queen gorgeous, she was also a Cordon Bleu cook, her fiancé was the governor of Georgia and she worked as spokesperson for a charity that educated severely injured kids. It was enough to nauseate the most generous of sisters.

But Cynthia was the undisputed genius of the family, and she usually tolerated Sabrina's perfection with amused equanimity.

"Cynthia, sweetie, I'm going to overlook that on the grounds that you're stressed," Sabrina said. "You can apologize when you're feeling better." A while back, Sabrina had called her sisters on their habit of gibing her; since then they'd both made an effort to give her the respect she deserved.

"Sorry," Cynthia muttered.

"Cyn, you okay?" Megan asked.

Cynthia took a healthy swig from the glass Sabrina handed her, and grimaced. "Fine. Dad said we should see him in his study."

"What about?" Megan asked.

"How would I know?" Cynthia snapped.

Megan caught Sabrina's eye. Her younger sister shook her head, mystified. Cynthia was famously even tempered.

The chairs in Jonah's study were occupied according to an unspoken and unchanging hierarchy: Cynthia took the wing chair closest to the desk, Megan sat in the matching armchair (without wings). Sabrina set a heavily watered down gin fizz on their father's desk, then curled up on the love seat.

Jonah leaned back in his padded leather chair behind the mahogany desk. His hair had turned entirely silver since the heart attack, making him look even more distinguished than he always had. "How's the Hoskins case going?" he asked Megan. "Who's the opposing counsel?"

"Travis Jamieson from Prescott Palmer."

"Jamieson?" Her father sounded perplexed rather than surprised.

"Do you know him?" Megan asked.

Jonah rubbed his chin. "Not really."

For the first time she could remember, she didn't believe her father. Her stomach felt suddenly hollow. "Dad, if there's something I should know..."

"There's nothing," he said sharply. He looked Megan in the eye. "I've never met the man."

The truth. Megan let out a shaky breath.

"I have some news—" Jonah addressed all of them "—that I want to share with you before it hits the grapevine. I've identified several people I consider possible candidates to head up Merritt, Merritt & Finch. A short list, if you will."

"Am I on it?" Megan's mouth ran away with her.

Sabrina made a little choking sound.

"You?" Cynthia said, evidently shocked that Megan should want to usurp a position that until recently had been hers. "But you don't have any commercial or criminal experience."

Gee, thanks, Cyn.

The gleam in her father's eye said he was ready for this battle. "Your sister's right." He steepled his fingers. "I hope to make an appointment by the new year, and to that end I've had preliminary discussions with Henry Whittington, Jack Loveridge III and Robert Grayson. They've each expressed an interest in the position."

All excellent lawyers, eminently qualified. If Dad hired any of those men, he'd have no need to consult Megan, to strategize with her. Heck, she'd be lucky if she ever saw him again, apart from at this weekly dinner.

"Dad, please—" she threw her pride to the wind and got ready to grovel in front of her sisters "—please at least consider me."

"You know what I think about that." Jonah slopped his gin fizz. He shook the drops off his hand, then took a slow sip. "Besides, sweetie, you work too hard."

Megan groaned inwardly—not that red herring again.

"You need some balance in your life," Jonah said.

"Dad, you're the workaholic in this family."

"And look where it got me." Her father thumped his chest.

"I'm a lot younger than you, and I'm in perfect health."

"You're setting up the habits of a lifetime right now," her father said. "In ten years' time, you won't be so young, or so healthy, and you'll be a sitting duck for a heart attack. You need more work-life balance." He looked as if he wanted to wash his own mouth out with soap, the way he had Megan's when she'd tried swearing when she was ten years old. The words *work-life balance* were a heresy to most lawyers.

"Cynthia's a workaholic, too," Megan said. "Do you tell her she needs more balance?" They all knew the answer to that.

"You're not your sister," Jonah said. "Cynthia has exceptional stamina."

"That's right." Cynthia traded a quick smile with Jonah.

Personally, Megan thought her sister looked exhausted, but she wasn't going to get anywhere by going head-to-head with her. "Dad, I have balance. I...I go to the movies with friends."

"Since *The Sound of Music*?" he demanded.

She rolled her eyes. "Of course." Although now that she thought about it, the last movie she'd seen might have been *Die Hard*. The first one.

"I go to the gym twice a week and I take a vacation every year." Her lawyer's instincts warned her not to give her father another excuse not to consider her for the job.

"How long since you had a date?"

"Three weeks," she said triumphantly. Thank goodness she'd accepted the offer of dinner from the opposing counsel she'd defeated in a recent case. She'd just about fallen asleep in her tiramisu, the evening was so dull, and so had he, but it still counted as a date. But if he'd kissed her good-night, she'd forgotten.

Her father grunted. "You need a steady boyfriend."

A nonlawyer boyfriend would dump her when he realized her attention was never fully on him, and any boyfriend who was a decent lawyer couldn't give her the attention she wanted.

"It would be nice if you found someone," Sabrina said. "You deserve a wonderful guy, Megan."

Sweet sentiment, lousy timing.

"I'm looking," Megan said. "*Actively* looking." Heck, she would promise to date a trapeze artist and have contortionist sex, if it would elevate her to Dad's short list.

Megan read doubt in her father's face, suspicion in Cynthia's, sympathy in Sabrina's. The room felt stifling, and she pushed herself to her feet.

"In fact, I have a date tonight. I'm going to the Hawks game. With a guy."

"What guy?" Cynthia and Jonah demanded simultaneously.

"Basketball?" Sabrina eyed her black suit and white blouse.

"Uh-huh. I need to go home and change."

THE MOMENT Megan got into her car, she phoned Travis. "I hope you didn't give away those Hawks tickets."

"Are you kidding? It'll be a great game, I'm on my way now."

"I'll see you there."

Silence at the other end.

"Unless your girlfriend is with you," she said, suddenly mortified.

"No girlfriend."

Warmth rushed through Megan. "Really? Even though you're so keen to get married?"

"Go figure," he said. "I have your ticket here, I'll meet you outside the gear store at seven."

"Seven, outside the store," she repeated, as she pulled out into the traffic.

"It's a date."

"It's not a date," she snapped, beset by the ridiculous thought that he could have read her mind, or overheard what she'd said to her father.

"Figure of speech," Travis said.

TRAVIS REALIZED two things when he met Megan outside the gear store at the arena, having executed a hasty juggle of his plans for the evening. First, he'd pictured her in his mind way more often than their professional association justified. Second, he'd pictured her in a variety of scenarios, but in none of them had she worn hip-hugging jeans, a tightish long-sleeved T-shirt and a baby-blue fleece jacket. The overall effect was undeniably cute.

She caught him staring. "What's wrong?"

"A Knicks cap?" He flicked the brim of her ball cap. "You'll be lynched by fans from both sides."

She shrugged. "I'm used to being the odd one out. I'll handle it."

"Yeah, but *I'll* have to look after you."

She frowned up at him from beneath the cap. "This is not a date."

"It's a business meeting." He feigned shock that she could even consider the possibility. "With hot dogs."

"Those things are bad for you," she said. But he caught a wistful note in her voice.

"Only if you eat more than six in one sitting." He was rewarded with a look of revulsion from her.

He was looking forward to tonight, and not just for the great basketball. The casual atmosphere of the arena was ideal to ask Megan a few questions.

He bought the hot dogs. One each. There would be fancier food served up in the club area, but for Travis, hot dogs were game food. Megan took hers without argument, then they headed for their seats.

It wasn't easy working their way through the crowd—the game was a sellout. As they reached the more expensive section, Travis realized half of Atlanta's top lawyers were here. The other half were probably being entertained in the private corporate suites.

The Hoskinses owned two fine seats—Megan's smirk said she knew just how lucky they were. Travis grinned and held her hot dog while she stowed her purse at her feet.

The game got off to a fast start, the Hawks' star player setting the pace with two slam dunks and a jump shot in the first quarter.

"They needed that," Megan said. The team's recent five-loss streak had been headline news.

"I didn't pick you for a basketball fan."

"And yet in our meeting with the Hoskinses, you thought I'd want to go the game."

"*I* wanted to go to the game," Travis corrected her. "I often come along with my dad." He scanned the field. "Our seats aren't usually quite as nice as these."

"I—" she broke off to applaud a layup shot by a player who'd just transferred into the Hawks from Chicago "—I'm still surprised you didn't bring a girlfriend."

"Your level of interest in my lack of a girlfriend seems excessive."

"Purely professional," she said snootily. "When a

good-looking guy tells a divorce lawyer he wants to get married and settle down, said divorce lawyer can't help calculating the odds of the marriage lasting."

"So cynical, for one so young," he marveled.

"Just planning my future income stream."

"You think if I got a divorce I'd hire you to represent me?"

"I'm not sure you'd be that smart," she said. "But your wife might."

He laughed. "Who've you chosen to represent *you* when you get divorced?"

"Who said I want to get married?"

"Do you?"

She fixed her gaze on the Hawks, huddled in a team time-out. From the cheaper seats, a couple of fans booed and yelled at them to hurry up, only not in such polite terms. "I've seen a lot of unhappy marriages, starting way back with my parents'."

Travis knew Jonah Merritt had married twice, but he didn't know the details. "Your folks split up?"

"Acrimoniously," she said. "I was only three, so I don't remember the ins and outs. But the bitterness lasted a long time."

"And that's put you off marriage."

The guy the other side of Megan put his fingers to his lips and issued a piercing whistle. Megan winced. "I'd need to be more certain than the average starry-eyed bride that I'd chosen the right guy. And I'd want an ironclad prenup."

"Ouch," he said. "How unromantic."

She shook her head. "Don't tell me you're a hearts-and-flowers guy. Naïveté doesn't qualify you to work at Prescott Palmer."

Travis scowled, but she met his gaze full on. "Yeah, you're right," he conceded. "I'm not sappy...but my parents have a great marriage. I want the same."

"I'm sure if you put a notice in the Law Journal you'd get dozens of applicants."

"No doubt your interest is still purely professional," he said, "but it seems you rate my attractions fairly high."

"I'm a reasonable judge." She scanned him. "I like to think I'm impartial."

Travis wasn't so sure about her impartiality, judging by the sparkle in her eyes. "I don't envisage my future wife being a lawyer," he said, to himself as much as to her.

"Let me guess, you want a doctor in the family to help you with those malpractice suits?"

He couldn't remember the last time a woman had made him laugh as much Megan did. "I'm thinking more a...homemaker."

Now it was her turn to laugh. Travis saw the moment she realized he was serious; her chin jerked back.

"Don't start on the chauvinist thing," he warned. "I know it's not politically correct, but you'll have noticed we at PPA seldom are. I don't care if everyone else rates their marriage on combined earning power, I've seen what works for our family."

A million questions jostled in Megan's eyes. But she pointed to the basketball court. "That was a foul."

She said nothing else until the end of the second quarter. They moved out into the aisle to stretch their legs.

"Megan," a man called.

Travis heard her groan under her breath as Robert

Grayson, a partner in one of the larger downtown law firms, picked his way down the crowded steps to them.

"Hi, Robert," she said, her voice neutral.

Grayson kissed her cheek. "I talked to your dad the other day. He seemed well."

The words were innocuous, but something in the searching glance he gave Megan put Travis on alert.

"I heard," she said with a tiny nod.

Grayson smiled. "How about you and I have dinner soon?"

Travis froze. Did Megan really know this guy? Know the things about him Travis did?

"Uh, maybe…" She glanced around as if she'd rather be anywhere else.

Travis stepped closer, so that his arm brushed hers. "We're pretty busy the next few weeks," he told Grayson.

The other man raised his eyebrows.

"Robert, this is Travis Jamieson," Megan said.

Robert offered a hand, so Travis shook it. "Jamieson…" The guy was obviously wondering if he should recognize the name.

"From Prescott Palmer," Megan said.

"You're with PPA?" Robert looked at Megan for confirmation.

Travis waited for her to clarify that they were working the same case, that this wasn't a date. She didn't say a word. That was weird, because he'd have bet money she would hate to be linked socially with a guy like him.

"I've been there ten years." Travis stared directly at Robert until the other man's distaste transformed into an awkwardness Megan wouldn't understand.

"We really should get together, Megan," Robert insisted. "I'll have my assistant call yours." He kissed her cheek again, which had the bizarre effect of curling Travis's hands into fists.

As he left, Megan glared after him.

"What was going on there? That was about more than dinner," Travis said.

She bit her lower lip in a way that made her seem curiously vulnerable. "I guess it won't hurt to tell you—it'll be all over town in a day or two."

"Lawyers are terrible gossips," he agreed. He took her by the elbow to steer her back to their seats.

"You've probably heard my dad plans to retire."

"Uh-huh." He stepped over someone's beer, and waited for her to do the same. They continued to edge along the row, squeezing past knees and backpacks.

"Dad's come up with a short list of people to replace him."

His head snapped around. "Already?" His urgency clearly surprised her. More calmly, he added, "I heard your father only decided a couple of weeks ago his heart can't take a return to the office."

She nodded. "Dad's a fast worker, even after a heart attack. He's made the search for his replacement a priority." She didn't sound happy about it. "I guess Robert wants to discuss the prospect of working together. He and I used to date."

Travis stopped, and she bumped into him, soft curves brushing against his arm. He shook off the distraction. "Did he hurt you?" he demanded.

She stared. "Of course he didn't—it just fizzled out. No hearts broken."

Travis had meant physically hurt, but he let it go.

He knew more than he cared to about Robert Grayson. He had to assume Jonah Merritt lacked the same knowledge. No way would he consider taking on a guy with that kind of secret in his past.

Grayson's innocent until proved guilty, Travis reminded himself.

They reached their seats as play resumed. "Do you think Grayson's the right guy to take over from your father?" he asked.

Megan shook her head.

Travis watched the fired-up Pistons work the ball down to the far end of the court. Without looking at Megan, he said, "Is there someone better on your dad's list?"

She seemed equally intent on the game. "No."

Two rebounds had the Pistons fans groaning.

"Your sister's not planning to quit her new job and come back to the firm?"

Annoyance flickered across her face. "No. Dad's set on Cynthia making judge."

"So you have no idea who should take over," he prompted.

At last he distracted her from the game.

"I didn't say that," she said shortly. "I don't think the firm needs to hire someone from outside."

Now things were getting interesting. "There's a good internal candidate?"

"An *excellent* internal candidate." Her lips—the ones he'd accidentally kissed and could still taste when he thought about it, which he did more than he should—flattened.

Travis felt as if he was wandering in one of Atlanta's famously thick fogs. Megan didn't want anyone from outside heading up Merritt, Merritt & Finch, and although there was an "excellent" internal person, she was unhappy…. The fog lifted.

"It's you," he said. "You want the job."

Around them, the crowd stood with a roar of approval. Megan stayed frozen in her seat. "No, I—"

"You want to run the firm." Travis knew he was right…but he could scarcely believe it. Cynthia Merritt was the daughter destined to run the company, everyone knew that. Megan Merritt was…a top-class lawyer, obviously. But quiet, unknown. Not on anyone's radar.

Not even on her father's if her black expression was any indication.

Hell. This complicated things. Travis raked a hand through his hair. The fans settled down around them.

"I don't want to talk about this," Megan said.

No argument from him. She clearly had no idea that Travis had sent his résumé to Jonah, that he'd tried to reach the man by phone several times, but couldn't get past his call-screening system. Travis had concluded the only way he could capture Jonah's attention was in court. He'd attended one of Megan's hearings in the hope her father would show up, had hung around in The Jury Room knowing she sometimes met her dad there. After he'd heard that Theo had appointed Megan, he'd badgered Barbara, knowing it was a big enough case for Jonah to take an interest.

Because Travis needed to impress Jonah Merritt. Fast. If he was to steer his life back onto the track he'd chosen years before, the track he'd slipped off when he'd done the wrong thing for the right reasons. Of course, he couldn't have guessed that choice would end up hurting his parents. Hell, it was hurting a whole town…

He glanced across at Megan, at her pinched expression. Dammit, he wasn't about to back down, just because she had some beef with her dad. He had to get that job.

CHAPTER FOUR

FAMILY COUNSELING WAS MEANT to be an attempt to save a marriage. Mr. and Mrs. Hoskins were using it as an opportunity to hammer home their respective custody claims.

It wasn't customary for lawyers to be present during counseling, but when Theo had ranted to Megan about the effect on their two children of his wife's lies about his drinking, she'd volunteered to come along and caution Barbara. It was above and beyond the call of duty, but the future business she might win from Theo was worth giving up any number of Saturdays. Plus, it might give her some inside information Travis didn't have.

Jeff Rawlings, the counselor, had asked to see the family in everyday action. The couple elected an outing to Centennial Park. They planned a walk, and then, while Jeff debriefed them, the kids would play in the playground. Megan could tell the counselor was less than thrilled to have her around, but he hadn't had much chance to voice his disapproval. He'd barely gotten a word in between the warring couple, who pinned smiles on their faces as they calmly fired salvos they hoped would "win" the session. Megan imagined her own parents, both lawyers, had fought with the same lethal precision.

"I admit I'm a busy professional," Barbara said in response to one of Theo's loaded comments as they skirted the Gold Medal Garden and headed toward the north pavilion and the ice rink that was set up in the park every winter. "But at least I'm a *sober,* busy professional."

"Hey!" Theo's courteous mask slipped; he grabbed his wife's elbow and loomed in her face.

"Mrs. Hoskins, any unsupported reference to an addiction may be viewed as defamation by the court." Megan issued her rapid warning in legalese, so as not to upset the Hoskins's son—ten years old, according to her notes—and his six-year-old sister. The children seemed focused on the ice rink up ahead, but she knew they would be trained to listen for the slightest discord.

After a long, strained moment, Theo let go of his wife's arm. "Thanks, Megan," he murmured, "I don't know what I'd do without you here. Probably strangle her."

Mercifully, he spoke too quietly for the kids—and the counselor—to hear, but the last thing Megan needed was her client threatening to kill his wife. She patted his shoulder and said, "I'm entirely at your service, Theo, so let's keep cool."

Barbara's calculating expression suggested she'd try to get her point across another way, one that didn't brush up against slander. She didn't succeed, and Megan issued a second warning five minutes later. This time, Theo held himself together. He was so grateful for her help, Megan wished she could whip out a commercial contract right now and ask him to sign on the dotted line.

"That's it," Barbara snapped. "You don't get to have your attorney here unless I do."

"Folks, this really isn't an occasion for lawyers," Jeff protested.

But Barbara was already punching a number into her cell phone.

Twenty minutes later, Travis ambled across the Great Lawn, ignoring the path the city had spent a fortune paving. It was clear he'd dropped whatever he was doing and come along without bothering to change. He wore boots, jeans and a faded blue sweatshirt that might have shrunk in the wash, judging by its snug fit across his broad shoulders. He carried a heavy gray wool jacket.

"Afternoon, all." He scanned the company, surely absorbing the tense atmosphere. His eyes met Megan's, then he studied her tailored cream pants and crimson coat. This was a client meeting, so she'd dressed appropriately, though less formally than she would have in the office. Not informally enough, according to Travis's knowing smile.

This is how reputable lawyers dress, she told him with her refusal to smile back. But he'd moved on to the kids. He hunkered down to their level and stuck out a hand. "Hi, I'm Travis."

"I'm Marcus." The boy pushed his glasses up his nose and shook Travis's hand. "This is Chelsea."

His sister, in a pink hat, scarf and gloves, offered a shy handshake.

Megan wasn't good with kids, so she hadn't tried to talk to them. Now, as Theo slung an approving arm around his son's shoulders, she felt as if Travis was showing her up. She smiled at Chelsea, and was rewarded with a solemn stare, unlike the smile the youngster had given Travis.

"Travis, the idea is for me to observe the family dynamics in action," Jeff Rawlings explained.

"Go right ahead," Travis said. "Megan and I are only here in case any legal boundaries get overstepped."

She'd already told the counselor that. She shoved her gloved hands into her coat pockets and glowered. The man had no idea how to behave in a business meeting. Though he was, she had to admit, good company at a basketball game.

Her mind wandered as Jeff informed the Hoskinses that at the end of the session, he would talk them through some opportunities for improvement based on his observations. She hadn't meant to tell Travis so much about her dad's retirement plans the other night. His lucky guess that she wanted to run the firm had made things awkward between them. At the end of the evening, he'd obeyed her earlier instruction and not attempted any kind of kiss. Thankfully.

Megan ran a finger across her lips, chapped by the cold air. Travis followed the movement, a thoughtful expression on his face. As if he might be contemplating kissing her.

More likely he was thinking about whoever he'd dated, *kissed*, last night.

He doesn't have a girlfriend, she reminded herself. She tuned into the counselor again.

He was trying to convince Mr. and Mrs. Hoskins to forget he was there. "Just do what you'd do on a regular family outing."

"Theo would normally play with his BlackBerry while I deal with the kids." Barbara's teasing tone might have fooled Marcus and Chelsea, but everyone else knew it for what it was: a well-aimed missile. Travis winced.

To Megan's relief, her client behaved himself. Theo pulled a fluorescent orange tennis ball from his pocket. "C'mon, kids, let's play ball tag." Without waiting for his wife's agreement, he jogged across the lawn, the kids close behind.

"Do you plan to join them, Barbara?" Jeff assessed Barbara's shoes: black pumps, heels probably four inches high. Megan always wore heels to work, but her feet ached just looking at those ankle-breakers.

"Of course." Barbara dug into her tote and produced a pair of sneakers. "The great thing about shoes is they come off. Unlike Theo's BlackBerry, which doesn't have an off button. And that, Ms. Merritt, is not defamation."

"Nor is it technically accurate," Megan pointed out. *So don't try saying it in court.*

Fifty yards away, Theo gave Marcus the tennis ball, appointing him "it." Theo grabbed Chelsea's hand, and father and daughter scampered away.

"He might look like a doting dad right now," Barbara said urgently to Jeff. "But at home he doesn't have five minutes for those kids."

They all watched Theo, whose enthusiasm seemed genuine enough to Megan. He let Marcus's poor throw hit him, then praised his son. Jeff smiled, nodded.

"Is this what the custody ruling will come down to?" Barbara demanded. "Which of us puts on a better show at tag? Because I don't do sports."

Megan sensed the woman's fear. The same fear she felt herself, when she worried she might inadvertently do something to ruin her chances with her father. She'd been known to snap at Trisha under that kind of pressure.

"I promise, it's not about tag," Travis said, with an easy reassurance that defused his client's panic.

"I love my kids," Barbara said to Jeff. "I'd die for them. How am I supposed to prove that?"

How am I supposed to prove I can run the firm? By making sure Theo outplayed Barbara in the divorce, then offered Merritt, Merritt & Finch his business, that was how. To achieve that, Megan might have to prove her client was the better parent.

Barbara's lowered head, her fierce concentration as she stuffed her feet into the sneakers, suggested that if she wasn't crying, she was on the verge.

"Barbara, I'm not here to judge you and Theo," Jeff said. Which wasn't entirely true. The counselor's report could be used in court to sway a custody argument.

Her head shot up. She was all dry-eyed disbelief. "For our next session, I get to choose the outing," she told Travis.

"You got it," he said. Megan opened her mouth to argue, then closed it. She could argue on Monday.

As Barbara trotted over to her family, Jeff moved beneath the shelter of the pavilion. He sat at a scarred picnic table and began taking notes.

Travis perched on the edge of the table, arms folded, watching the Hoskinses. "Wouldn't it be great if counseling convinced Theo and Barbara to stick together?"

Megan edged onto the seat the other side of the table from Jeff. "I know you have an idealistic view of marriage, but even you can't seriously think that'll happen."

"I said it would be *great*, not likely."

Jeff shook his pen, which wasn't working properly on the rough surface. "If people came to counseling before they started talking to lawyers, they might have a chance."

Across the lawn, Barbara's arrival had changed the group dynamic. Even from here, Megan picked up on the stiffening of Theo's posture, the careful distance Barbara kept from him. If the couple's allegations about each other were true, then they were both hurting…but neither of them betrayed their vulnerability. Megan didn't blame them. In law, attack was often the best form of defense.

But when kids were involved, surely the rules should change. *Should.*

Tag segued into a game of catch, maybe in concession to Barbara's claimed inability to "do" sports. After a few lackluster rounds, Marcus dropped the ball, earning a tactless rebuke from his dad. The boy burst into tears, no doubt in response to the tension between his parents as much as anything. Barbara stuck her hands on her hips and shot a look at the counselor before she swept Marcus into her arms.

Hovering impotently outside the mother-son embrace, Theo didn't notice that Chelsea had sat down on the cold grass.

"Do you see what's going on?" Megan asked Jeff. "Barbara's using her son to score points with you." Her earlier sympathy evaporated; she wanted to slap the woman.

Perhaps from the combination of cold and her brother's distress, Chelsea started to cry, loud, attention-seeking sobs. Theo hurried over to help her up, brushing grass off her bottom. Eventually, the ball game resumed, with both parents on their best behavior, which seemed to dampen the kids' enjoyment even more.

"Mind if I lighten things up a bit?" Travis asked the counselor.

Jeff shrugged. "Go ahead."

Travis left his jacket on the table and ran to join the family. He seemed to be explaining some new game.

When he wove a zigzag path across the lawn, Megan realized he'd set up a kind of reverse tag, where everyone else was "it," and he was the target. The kids aimed the tennis ball at him, shrieking as he danced and dodged among them.

The game wrapped up soon after, and the atmosphere was notably lighter as the Hoskinses served cookies and hot chocolate to the children in the pavilion.

"Nice work," the counselor said to Travis.

"You've played with kids before," Megan said, trying not to feel miffed that he'd proved more effective with the children.

"My nephews." Travis batted damp grass from his jeans. "I love spending time with them."

Hence his desire to settle down and have kids. With a homemaker wife. A shared recollection of that conversation flashed between them.

Megan dropped her gaze to the counselor's notebook. What had he written about her client's parenting techniques? She needed to brush up on her upside-down reading.

After the snack, Jeff announced he would discuss his observations with Barbara and Theo, along with solutions to any problems they felt needed addressing. Travis leaned into Megan and murmured, "The chances of this conversation staying peaceful are zilch, don't you agree?"

His warm breath fanned her face, a distraction that slowed her processing of what he'd said. Eventually, she nodded.

Travis stood. "Kids, how about we go ice-skating?"

Chelsea clapped her hands.

"Cool," Marcus said.

"Is it okay to take them to the rink?" Travis asked their parents.

"That would be great, thanks," Theo said. "These guys love to skate."

The kids took off toward the ice, while Travis shrugged into his jacket. "Coming?" he asked Megan.

"Thanks, but I'm needed here." It was idiotic to feel as if she should have had the idea to suggest skating. Theo needed her here as a lawyer, not a babysitter.

"I'll be fine," Theo assured her. "I'd appreciate if you could help with the kids."

Okay, so her star client *did* need her as a babysitter. "No problem," she said smoothly, aware that once again, she'd provoked Travis's amusement.

At the rink, Travis rented skates for the kids and himself. He turned to Megan. "What size are you?"

"Me? I'm not skating. I'm still bruised from last time, and that was five years ago." Her hands went to her butt. She wasn't about to risk giving her client reason to doubt her competence, not even in an activity unrelated to her work.

"Baby," Travis scoffed. He laced Chelsea's skates and checked Marcus's self-lacing. "I'll catch up to you," he told the kids, who stumbled over their feet in the rush to hit the ice.

He sat on the concrete bench and pulled off his left boot to reveal a thick, black wool sock. "So, was it your idea to ruin my Saturday?" He shoved his foot into a skate and began threading the laces.

"I didn't ask you to come along."

"I have a feeling Theo didn't ask *you*, either," he said. "I think you offered, out of your eagerness to be the best lawyer in town and impress your dad."

She tugged the lapels of her coat together, hands beneath her chin. "Theo needed me, so I was here for him." She sounded defensive even to her own ears. Consciously, she let go of her coat, allowing her hands to hang loose. "Besides, it got me away from the tedious task of checking the invitation list for the firm's Christmas party."

"Nothing better to do on the weekend than work, huh?"

He was teasing, but it was so close to the truth.... Megan fixed her gaze on the children, messing around on the ice while they waited for him.

"You do realize," Travis said, "the way to a client's heart is through his kids?"

"What do you mean?"

"People have no objectivity when it comes to their children," he said. "If you're kind to the rug rats, they assume you're a wise and wonderful person all-around."

"Is that why you're so charming to Marcus and Chelsea?" she demanded, outraged.

"Could be." He tapped his nose. "If you don't want to lose points with Theo, I suggest you get your skates on."

She stomped over to the kiosk and asked for some skates, then tugged off her black fur-trimmed woolen gloves, freeing her fingers for the laborious process of lacing up.

"Cute socks," Travis said, when she removed her ankle boots to reveal the lime-green-and-watermelon-striped socks Sabrina had given her. She ignored him.

When she was done, she forced her chilled fingers back into her gloves and stood up gingerly, adjusting to the change in balance.

"Last one on the ice is a sleazy lawyer," Travis taunted, and stepped confidently onto the white-gray rink.

Megan pounded and scratched her way across the ice with her first, clumsy steps. She would have liked to hug the edge for a while, but she got the hang of the push-slide motion and made it, with some wobbling, to the center of the rink. At first, all that was required of her and Travis was to applaud enthusiastically as Marcus and Chelsea performed tricks.

After ten minutes, during which Megan found her balance and made a few practice turns, Travis set Marcus a challenge of skating ten lengths without falling over. "Six lengths for you, Chelsea, with one of your super-duper twirls at each end." The children whooped as they raced away.

"How do you know so much about kids?" Megan said. "Can't just be from having nephews." Some parents never got a handle on their own children, never realized that one size didn't fit all.

Travis shrugged. "My family's close, I see a lot of the boys—or the little terrors, as we call them. Whenever I take Luke camping, Davey insists I owe him a sleepover at my place here in town. Mom says it's fitting punishment for running rings around her when I was that age."

The love in his voice as he talked about his family was a nice quality in a guy, Megan realized.

She skated in the children's wake, her blades now making the smooth sound they should. Travis easily kept pace.

"You're pretty good," he said. "I ought to sue you for skating under false pretences—I'd hoped to be massaging your butt by now."

"You've just guaranteed I'll stay on my feet."

"Too bad."

She bit back a smile. "I like skating, although I did have a bad fall five years ago. It's the anticipation that's nerve-racking, I'm fine once I get going."

"Kind of like sex," he mused.

Megan stumbled, almost fell. Travis grasped her elbow. "Steady, or you'll be up for that massage."

She was tempted, for one moment, to lean into his strength. "Quit it," she said, tugging free. "The children will hear."

"Yes, ma'am."

The kids were a good thirty yards away. As they watched, Chelsea slipped and fell, but with Marcus's help she got up laughing.

"They're lucky to have each other," Megan said. "It'll help them keep faith in their family."

"You're speaking from experience," Travis guessed.

They were gaining on the youngsters; Megan slowed down. She focused on the glide of her right skate, then her left. "I was too young to remember the specifics of my parents' arguments, but you don't forget the anger, the bitterness. That stuff seeps right into the walls and floorboards."

"No wonder you're cynical about marriage."

She shot him a long-suffering look. "Better cynical than deluded. Where do you plan to find your home-maker wife?"

CHAPTER FIVE

Now there was a question he hadn't anticipated. Travis glanced around, as if the love of his life might be knitting a sweater nearby. "I've been wondering that myself." With a greater sense of urgency over the past few months, ever since his life in Atlanta had run smack into his parents' lives in Jackson Creek, precipitating his quest for respectability. It was like hanging one of those black velvet clown paintings next to a Rembrandt portrait.

"You could marry a twenty-year-old," Megan suggested. "One who hasn't chosen a career yet and will think dropping out of college to do your laundry isn't too horrible."

He almost welcomed her implication that his dream of a traditional family was preposterous. "That sounds kinda creepy, given I'm thirty-five. Besides, I like a woman with an education."

"So, you're looking for a woman who has a college degree but doesn't want to use it?"

She was right; it was absurd. He laughed.

"It really bugs you, doesn't it, that I want to marry a homemaker?" He couldn't begin to imagine her reaction to the news that having the life he'd imagined required him to chase after the same job she wanted.

"I find it fascinating." Megan executed a fancy little two-step on her blades, sending up a fine spray of water from the ice.

"Show-off," he said. He skated ahead, then turned to face her. Which meant skating backward. Two could play at the show-off game. "Here's a thought," he said, as much to himself as to her. "How about I find a woman who has a college degree and a few years under her belt in a job she enjoys. Then I ask her to give up her career."

Megan gaped. Not, he guessed, at his backward skating prowess.

"She won't have to stop working right away," Travis said. "Not until we have kids."

"How about you give up *your* career?" she suggested. "You could look after the kids while your wife works."

He rubbed his chin. "Interesting concept, but ultimately unsatisfying for my primal male need to be the family provider." That was only half a joke.

From the gleam of anticipation in her eyes, he gathered he was about to collide with someone. He turned just in time to dodge a teenage boy who was skating in a T-shirt.

"Thanks for the warning," he murmured to Megan. She grinned, so unguarded that he had the urge to grab her hands and dance with her on the ice.

"Good luck with finding someone to take you up on your highly resistible marriage offer," she said.

She had a point. Travis tended to date career women, because those were the women he met. He had yet to find one he wanted to ask to give up her job to raise their kids, but when he did, he supposed she might think it an unreasonable request. On the other hand, maybe, when he met the right woman, it wouldn't seem unreasonable at all. He had a fleeting image of Megan standing in his kitchen, wearing an apron, a toddler at her feet.

"What are you smirking at?" she asked.

"I hope to marry a woman who wants more from life than work," he said.

"Let me guess, she'll want the privilege of raising your children?" she mocked.

They were near the corner of the rink; Travis skated to the fence. Megan came to a stop beside him. "I do believe raising children is a privilege," he said. "For both parents, whether they're working or not."

He'd managed to silence her. After a moment, she jerked her head in a nod. "You're right."

"Always," he said, lifting the mood again. "It's not all one-sided, you know, my *resistible offer*. There will be compensations for my wife giving up her career. Such as a husband who knows she and the kids are more important than any career ambition, who's loyal and faithful." He paused. "And of course, we'll have incredible sex."

She slithered against the fence, caught herself, and said calmly, "Incredible is a subjective term, Counselor. One learns not to trust subjectivity."

"You'd rather I produce an expert witness?" He enjoyed the roll of her eyes more than he would have any flirtatious rejoinder. It occurred to him he'd enjoy proving the veracity of his claim to her even more.

Whoa. He edged away from her along the fence. Contemplating kissing her was one thing, thinking bed was something else entirely.

"How can you have such faith in your ideal marriage when you see couples like the Hoskinses?" Megan followed him, and from the purposeful thrust of her skates she sensed she had him on the run. Travis hoped she hadn't figured out exactly what was making him uncomfortable. "Theo and Barbara probably started off just as starry-eyed."

Travis kept up his slow, backward skating along the fence line as he checked on the kids: they'd teamed up with a boy about Chelsea's age and were playing tag on the ice. "I'm not sure everyone enters marriage with the idea that family will always come first. But you see a lot more divorces than I do, you're the expert."

"I struggle with the idea of a divorce lawyer who believes in the fairy tale," she admitted, gliding along at the same snail's pace he was.

"I'm not suggesting the wave of a wand will get me what I want," he said. "It'll take hard work, and there are no guarantees. One of my brothers is divorced."

She gasped in mock horror.

"In Clay's defense," he said, "the reason they divorced is because his wife's career required her to spend three nights a week in the city. She found someone else."

"Her career killed the marriage," Megan intoned.

"Pretty much. Now Clay has full custody of the boys, and Laura barely sees them."

She swatted his arm, and despite her glove, Travis felt the contact as a flash of heat through the late afternoon chill.

"Careers don't kill marriages," she said. "People do."

"No need to make it harder than it has to be." He

glanced over his shoulder to check he wasn't on a collision course. The skaters were thinning out as dusk fell.

"That's why people should think twice before they have children," she muttered.

"Or work twice as hard at getting it right when they do."

She shook her head. "I'd like to get married one day, but I don't plan on having kids."

"What, never?" Travis stopped abruptly, and Megan's blades clashed with his, toe-to-toe. "You just haven't met the right guy to father them. Or your biological clock hasn't started ticking." Megan didn't strike him as being like Laura, his ex-sister-in-law. Then again, Clay had never dreamed his wife would consider kids a hindrance.

Megan disentangled their skates. "My job requires a huge commitment, one I want to give. It would be hard enough making room for a husband—I don't think I should have kids if I can't spare the effort to be the best parent possible."

"Good argument," he admitted. "You should be a lawyer." Their skates were no longer touching, but she was still very close to him. He eyed the curve of her mouth. The contrast between the no-nonsense top lip and the tempting fullness of her lower lip struck him as inordinately sensual. Which either meant he hadn't dated in too long, or his brain had frozen over. Because Megan was the exact opposite of what he wanted. Next time he came skating, he'd wear a hat.

"What does your boyfriend think about your lack of interest in having kids?" he asked.

"I don't have a boyfriend."

"You're kidding."

Megan rolled her eyes again. She seemed to have trouble believing in her own attractions; Travis had the urge to educate her. Thoroughly. Probably the onset of hypothermia, he told himself halfheartedly.

She pushed away from the fence, headed for the center of the ice. Over her shoulder, she said, "The way I'm going, the kids question won't even come up. I haven't yet found a man who's more exciting than my career."

Some perverse instinct had him skating after her, faster than she was going. He passed her, and spun quickly, forcing her to stop. "Then you're dating the wrong guys."

"Dating advice from a divorce lawyer—why didn't I think of that earlier?" She skated around him.

Drop it, he ordered himself. *You're not here to talk about your love life, or hers.* He fell in beside her and they skated toward the children. "Why do you want to run your dad's firm? Your family law division is growing fast, I hear. Why do you want the headache of looking after criminal and corporate as well?"

Megan's sidelong squint suggested she wished she could deny she'd ever wanted the top job at Merritt, Merritt & Finch. "It's a logical next step."

"I'm sensing more emotion than logic."

"It's about family, you should understand that. The whole firm's important to Dad, especially the corporate practice, so it's important to me." She folded her arms across her chest. A risky pose when ice skating, but she seemed in full control.

"Too bad he won't give you the job."

She skated ahead. "I have a plan that ought to change his mind."

Travis hoped not. Right now, he was an even less credible candidate than she was in Jonah Merritt's eyes. But he intended to upgrade his status. Fast.

So, it seemed, did she.

He wasn't worried about proving himself against the likes of Robert Grayson. But if Megan worked her way onto that list...she would be formidable competition. He felt his way with his next question. "Why doesn't your father think you can run the firm?" So far, Travis had no clue what it would take to impress the man.

She wove through a group of teenagers. Travis followed. "Dad says I don't command the respect of the partners...though I'm sure I could if I had to."

That would count against Travis, too. "Is that all?"

"He's not convinced I can bring in new clients across the other divisions," she added. "For all that he's a traditional lawyer, Dad has a mile-wide sales streak. He's responsible for more new business than anyone else."

Business development was a particular strength of Travis's. He'd mentioned that in his one-sided correspondence with Jonah, but even that hadn't been enough to secure an interview. The stigma of working for PPA outweighed all other considerations. On the plus side, at PPA you learned how to find creative routes to what you wanted.

"I've always admired your father," Travis said. It was true, so why should his conscience prick? "There aren't many firms where the founding partner exerts so much influence over such a long time."

"No mortal could oust my dad," she said wryly. "Sadly for him, a heart attack is no respecter of men."

"I've never actually met him," Travis said. "Is he as

impressive in real life as his reputation suggests?" The question sounded stilted to his own ears, but Megan didn't bat an eyelid.

"More so," she said fondly. "I'll introduce you one day."

Exactly what he'd been angling for. Before Travis could pin her down to a time and date, Marcus and Chelsea skated over.

"Did you see me do a jump?" Marcus asked.

"Like a pro," Travis said. *Tomorrow.* He ran through his schedule. It would take some maneuvering, but tomorrow he would pin Megan down to that introduction to her dad.

"PRETTY." Chelsea pointed to the trees, where the fairy lights twinkled in the deepening dusk. Her teeth chattered through her smile.

Megan chafed the girl's arms through her fleece jacket. "They're lovely, like Christmas trees."

Chelsea began a complicated monologue about Christmas and Santa Claus that involved naming at least a dozen reindeer. Megan uh-huhed politely, but her mind wandered to Merritt, Merritt & Finch, to her father and his assumption she couldn't bring in new clients for the other divisions. If she could just convince Theo to hand over a chunk of his legal business… Frustrated, she tipped her head back to look at the sky. The rising moon sat low still, a pale sliver of its full self. About as substantial as Megan's hopes of getting that job.

"Looks like Barbara and Theo are done." Travis pointed at the couple making their way toward the ice rink. "It's getting late, kids, let's call it a day."

Megan's cell phone rang as the children were putting on their shoes. Robert Grayson.

"Robert, how are you?"

Beside her, Travis stiffened. "Tell him to get lost," he ordered. As if she was one of his spineless home-maker girlfriends with no mind of her own.

"Great to hear from you." She spoke a lot more warmly to Robert than she had the other night.

"I enjoyed our chat at the game." The man had clearly picked up on her friendly vibe. "I meant what I said about dinner—how about Monday?"

Why would she want to have dinner with him, when in all likelihood he wanted to butter her up to support his application for *her* job? On the verge of refusing, it occurred to Megan it might be interesting to know what her dad had said to Robert.

"Dinner Monday?" she repeated. "Excellent idea." Travis's darkening expression as he snapped Chelsea's hood back onto her jacket where it had come loose was an added bonus. What made him think he was an expert on her personal life?

"I thought we could go to Chez Martine." A luxuri-ous, overly formal restaurant in Buckhead. "Or maybe Salt."

"I love Salt," Megan said, to rub *salt* in Travis's hopefully wounded ego. "Let's go there."

That was a hiss from Travis, if she wasn't mistaken. To remind him whose life this was, she accepted Robert's offer to pick her up at her apartment. Unfor-tunately, the greedy note in his voice as he said goodbye suggested he'd jumped to the same conclusion Travis was intended to—that this was a date. She would call him later and arrange to meet him at the restaurant.

"You're going on a date with Grayson?" Done with Chelsea's hood, Travis loomed over Megan, brows drawn together, mouth set in a scowl.

"For all you know, that was my elderly uncle Robert," she said coolly.

"It was Grayson," he snapped.

Hmm, so the laid-back Travis Jamieson was capable of getting riled. She filed that away as potentially useful in the courtroom. "If you say so."

"He's not the right guy for you."

"Butt out, Travis," she ordered…and realized Marcus and Chelsea were staring at them, their faces drawn and tense. She forced a smile. "Sorry, kids, I always get grouchy when I'm hungry."

She saw rather than heard Travis's stifled curse. He winked at the children, grinned. "And I always get bossy around a beautiful woman."

Chelsea giggled, but she still looked tense. In the interest of peace, Megan decided to overlook the chauvinistic slant to his comment.

"We'd better get back to Mom and Dad." Marcus shoved his hands in his pockets and slouched in the direction of his parents.

Megan knew exactly what he was thinking. That grown-ups were mean and unfair, making kids miserable with their fighting. How could she, of all people, have been so thoughtless?

Barbara and Theo arrived, walking side by side but with about six feet of space between them.

"Did you have a good time, guys?" Theo scooped Chelsea up; she wrapped her arms around his neck.

"It was cool," Marcus reported. "Travis can skate backward."

"Great stuff," Theo said heartily. The way he was avoiding looking at his wife suggested the counseling session hadn't gone well. The children would see through their dad's heartiness, Megan knew.

"I saw you skating, sweetheart," Barbara said to Chelsea. "You were wonderful." Chelsea reached for her mom, and after a brief hesitation, Theo passed her over.

"Thanks, Travis." Theo shook his hand. "The kids needed some fun." Megan suspected that was a dig at his wife as much as a compliment to Travis. "You, too, Megan," he added belatedly.

"Anything I can do," Megan murmured.

"You're not the first to say I make a better babysitter than a lawyer," Travis joked. It was the kind of self-deprecating comment that made men look good and women look feeble. Theo said something about the relative value of babysitters and lawyers, and in short order the two men had a males-only conversation going on.

Megan was wary of the respect in Theo's eyes as he spoke to Travis. She wouldn't put it past Travis to be plotting some PPA-style underhandedness. Such as trying to snaffle some of Theo's business for his firm. *Not on my watch.*

Chelsea wiped her nose on her sleeve, transferring a string of clear snot. Barbara handed her a tissue. "Didn't Daddy see you needed to blow?"

As his sister blew into the tissue, Marcus blinked hard and hunched his shoulders.

Megan remembered doing the same thing herself years ago. Remembered how no amount of blinking and hunching could protect a kid from hurt.

She groped for the calm she usually brought to her work. She had enough on her mind without worrying about the Hoskins kids, or about Travis stealing her client.

She needed to follow the advice she'd given Theo, to keep cool. Tomorrow, back in the office, she would get her head together, plan a way forward that would allow her to focus on what really mattered.

Convincing her dad she should have that job.

MEGAN STARTED Monday morning with a seven o'clock meeting to agree on the final touches for Merritt, Merritt & Finch's famous Christmas bash. As the only Merritt currently employed at the firm, she was head of the party committee. In theory, that meant signing off on a long list of recommendations.

In reality, the party was a big deal to her father, and she found it impossible to let even the smallest decision go unchallenged. The committee members—lawyers and admin staff—would doubtless hate her by the time the big night arrived. But it was worth being pedantic to get it right, she assured herself, as she overturned the salmon canapés decision in favor of the turkey and cranberry roulade.

From eight, she had client meetings scheduled through to midday, which made twelve o'clock the first opportunity she had to call Travis.

He must have had her number programmed into his cell phone, because he answered with, "Megan, hi." The unexpectedness of hearing her name in his deep, sexy voice made her stomach lurch.

"I was about to call you," he said. There was no trace of his previous annoyance at the prospect of her dating Robert. That was good, of course.

"I assume you received a copy of the counselor's report?" she asked, her voice crisp.

"It's probably at my office. I'm taking the morning off."

"Excuse me?"

He chuckled. "Surely a morning off isn't entirely outside your frame of reference?"

"Of course not." Her gaze measured the mile-high stack of files on her desk. She doubted Travis could have any fewer. Then it clicked for her. "I'm sorry, Travis, is it a funeral?"

He laughed. "There are other reasons to take a morning off, Megs. I promise you, no one died."

Megs? No one called her that. Why was he so friendly after their disagreement on Saturday. What was he after?

"Although things don't look too hot for the old guy in the blue bathrobe," he continued.

"What on earth are you talking about?"

"The book I'm reading. No one's died, but the title is *Silence in the Tomb.* I figure it's only a matter of time."

"You took time off work to read a thriller?" She hoped she didn't sound as rattled as she felt. Did Travis think he was so much better than she was that he didn't even have to *try* to win the case? *Or maybe my strategy of encouraging him to underestimate me is working big-time.*

"This is a mystery," he said, affronted. "I don't read thrillers."

Megan had no idea what the difference was. On the rare occasions she read fiction, she usually tried to catch up with whatever had won the Pulitzer or the Nobel

Prize. She retreated to solid ground. "The counselor sent over a report this morning, recommending two more sessions. He doesn't feel either Theo or Barbara was entirely honest during Saturday's meeting."

"Not a surprise," Travis said. Over the phone she heard the blare of a car horn. Was he reading outdoors? She eyed the gray sky outside her window. She suspected Travis would read in the rain if the fancy took him. How odd that he should be so disturbingly unconventional in some ways, yet so traditional in his views about family.

"I assume you and I will be asked to attend those extra sessions, if only to babysit." She tackled the easier of her two missions first. "I want us to agree not to argue in front of Marcus and Chelsea. Those kids hear enough of that from their parents. We should show them that adults can live in harmony."

He hummed a few bars of "Ebony and Ivory." "Let me get this straight. You're saying you and I should act happily married?"

She leaned back in her chair and crossed her ankles, aware he was disarming her. That was okay; disarming went both ways, and she could pick up her weapons anytime. She loosened her grip on the phone. "Polite and respectful will provide sufficient contrast between us and their parents."

"Good idea. For someone who doesn't like kids, you've given this some serious thought." The cadence of his voice had changed; it sounded as if he was on the move. Maybe that mystery novel was an audiobook. A dull rumble of traffic filled the pause.

"I never said I don't like children, just that I don't want to have them." She twisted the phone cord in her fingers. "The look on the Hoskins kids' faces after you and I snapped at each other...I lay awake half the night."

"Did you now?" His voice dropped to a low, suggestive pitch that sent a frisson through her.

She straightened up. *Dammit, where did I put my armor?*

"Look out your window," Travis said.

Megan heard the whine of a bus's brakes in her ear. She shoved her chair back and made her way around the desk, phone in hand. The stretched phone cord knocked the penholder off her desk; pens, paper clips and a Hi-Liter cascaded to the carpet.

From her third-floor vantage point, well above the traffic, Travis was easily visible among the thronging pedestrians on the other side of the road. He had his cell phone to his ear and with his other hand he waved a paperback at her. "Come on down," he invited her. "I'll buy you a sandwich."

Megan knuckled her temples. "What are you doing outside my building?"

"Asking you to lunch," he said patiently.

How was she supposed to plan a strategy, when he never did what she expected? She weighed her options. She could refuse, and warn him over the phone against muscling in on her client. But after all that talk of hors d'oeuvres this morning and with no court appearances planned today, she was hungry and a little stir-crazy. Face-to-face, she could stake her claim on Theo in no uncertain terms.

"It's not that big a decision, Megs," Travis teased, still in that suspiciously friendly tone.

She hung up. *Keep him guessing, even if it's only for five minutes.*

TRAVIS TOOK HER to a sandwich bar on Central. He ordered the roast beef sandwich; Megan chose an egg salad wrap. She gathered cutlery and a couple of napkins from the baskets on the counter.

"Coffee?" Travis offered.

"Espresso, thanks," she said automatically.

"Two lattes," he told the girl serving behind the counter.

Megan's jaw dropped; she snapped her mouth shut. Only to open it again. "Did you hear what I said?"

"If you think I can enjoy my latte while you sit there making eyes at it, like you did at our meeting last week…"

"I didn't make eyes at your coffee." How did Travis see things no one else could?

"You must have been making them at me, then."

She tightened her grip on the knives and said through gritted teeth, "You're delusional."

"My mistake, Counselor." He smirked.

The only person making eyes around here was the server, gawking at Travis as if he was the best thing since cappuccino.

Unwilling to make a scene—who knew how many of the people in here were lawyers?—Megan stalked to the only spare table in the place. Travis joined her a minute later, carrying their coffees. She tried not to look too entranced at the sight of the frothy lattes—hers with cream on top, damn him.

He set the drinks on the table and sat on the slatted wooden chair opposite her. He wore faded jeans and a gray sweatshirt, and beneath the sweatshirt, she got a glimpse of white T-shirt. Crazy that such ordinary clothes could combine to look so ruggedly masculine.

She wondered if he knew the effect he had on her. Undoubtedly. Which made her wonder if it was calculated. "Why were you reading outside my building?"

He wedged the card with their order number into the flower-shaped metal holder. "I wasn't. I was a block away at Cameron Hospital. My dad's in town for a post-op consultation, so I took the morning off to go along with him. Figured I'd earned it, after someone made me work Saturday."

She ignored the dig about Saturday. "I hope your dad's condition isn't serious."

He stirred sugar into his coffee. "Hip replacement, all by the book. I left Dad waiting for the doc and told him I'd hang out here until he's done. He should be another hour."

"I'll be gone by then."

Travis read relief in the infinitesimal shift of Megan's shoulders. The feeling was mutual. He had a reason for this meeting, and it wasn't to introduce her to his dad.

The exact opposite, in fact. It was to secure an introduction to *her* father. And he'd realized just how to get it after he arrived home on Saturday. Megan had planted the idea when she mentioned she was vetting the invitation list to the celebrated Merritt, Merritt & Finch Christmas party. It was the most prestigious event of the year, attended by senior Merritt, Merritt & Finch staff, judges, corporate clients and selected members of the legal fraternity…including a handful of lawyers from other firms. Jonah Merritt presided over the occasion every year, without fail.

All Travis had to do was get himself invited, then make sure he met Jonah there. Once they were talking face-to-face, he was sure he could convince Jonah to interview him.

First, he had to persuade Megan to invite him. Which should be no skin off her nose, since she was ignorant of his motives.

Travis studied her face—including that small, straight nose—then moved down to the champagne-colored silk blouse she'd paired with a forest-green tweed skirt.

"For someone who lay awake half the night worrying about the Hoskins kids you look great," he said. "Add a red scarf to that outfit and you could be one of Santa's elves." Might as well bring the conversation around to the holiday season.

"How tacky," Megan said, and he grinned, eliminating flattery as a persuasion technique.

Their sandwiches arrived; they juggled salt, pepper and ketchup and mustard to make room on the table. Travis bit into his beef sandwich, while Megan partially unrolled her wrap to scrutinize the contents.

"Okay?" He watched her careful inspection. Would pursuing his desire to meet Jonah arouse her suspicions? It didn't matter if it did, since she wasn't in the running. In which case, why not he tell her outright he wanted the job? *Not going there.*

"It seems fine." She rewrapped her lunch securely. "How's your coffee?"

Despite the longing in her tawny eyes, she was clearly determined not to give him the satisfaction of drinking it. He waited. At last, she picked it up and sipped, her eyes closed in appreciation.

The way they would be if he kissed her. *Hell.*

Megan's eyes snapped open. "Ugh." She clattered the cup back onto the table.

"What's the problem?" Travis steadied the cup, wobbling precariously in its saucer.

"It tastes awful," she said. "Like reheated dishwater."

He sampled his own. "Mine's fine." He slid his cup toward her. "Try it."

One swallow, and she rejected his as well. "Yech. It's so milky."

"*Latte* being the Italian for milk," he said.

"I don't think they even put any coffee in." She sniffed hers as if she suspected him of poisoning her. "I don't believe it. All these years, I've hankered after a latte—" she pushed her cup away and eyed him accusingly "—and I don't like it."

"You've wanted a latte for *years?* Why the hell didn't you just order one?"

She picked up her wrap and took a bite. "You said you were going to call me this morning. Was it about Theo?"

"Tell me about your coffee hang-up."

Her fingers tightened around her wrap. The filling bulged; a chunk of egg salad dropped onto her plate. "Nothing to tell. Have you spoken to Theo since Saturday afternoon?"

"You're obviously not lactose intolerant."

She dabbed at her mouth with her napkin. "I want to know what you're up to."

"Are you afraid of froth?"

It was a throwaway remark, meaningless. But her fingers twitched, dislodging more egg salad. *Afraid of froth.* No such phobia. But the answer was in there somewhere. Travis glanced from the coffee, the whipped cream now melting over the sides of the cup, back to Megan's set, intense expression.

"What does your father drink?" he asked.

"Stop changing the subject. You're hiding something."

A warning bell went off in his brain; he ignored it. "A thousand bucks says it's espresso." Then inspiration struck. "On second thought, I'll let you off easy—an invitation to your firm's Christmas party says Jonah Merritt drinks espresso." *Yes*.

"What if he does?" she said.

"You order the same drink as your dad, while your eyes beg for a latte. The word *froth* gets you agitated…"

"You're crazy. Either that, or you'll say anything to avoid answering my questions."

"You think your father wouldn't take you seriously if you ordered frothy coffee?"

"Why are you obsessing about coffee?" But her voice shook, and he knew he was right.

"You can't seriously believe your dad would think less of you if you drank lattes."

"You can't seriously believe your ravings about coffee will stop me noticing your little scheme."

Her sharp tone arrested him. "What scheme?"

"You've been acting strangely ever since I called you."

He drew back. "Garbage."

She crumpled her serviette. "You have some agenda I don't know about."

How had she reached that conclusion? One look at her eyes revealed the keen intelligence there. Her brain had been working just as fast as his, in a different direction. And somehow she'd picked up on his ulterior motive. *I want to meet your father. I want the job you think should be yours. I want to salvage the life I planned.*

The hell he would admit to any of that. He gulped down his latte as he cast around for something to say, knowing an outright denial would only cause her to probe further. *Do something, before she figures it out.*

Slowly, deliberately, he set his cup in its saucer. "I want you to cancel your date with Robert Grayson."

CHAPTER SIX

ROBERT? He was worried about her dinner with Robert? Megan had been so tightly poised to pounce on a denial, to worry at it until Travis caved in, that now she felt as if she was teetering on a cliff edge.

"You are way out of line." But her words lacked heat as she considered and discarded reasons he might have said what he did. Reasons like, Travis was jealous because he wanted to date her himself; he was jealous because he wanted to date Robert himself; he was worried Robert might give her good advice about the Hoskins case; Robert knew something unsavory about Travis, and Travis was afraid she would discover it and it would prejudice his case.... Yes! That had to be it.

Behind her, a male voice spoke into the shocked silence. "Now I see why you were so keen to abandon your father in the emergency ward."

Megan twisted in her chair, to see an older version of Travis smiling down at her.

"You were nowhere near the emergency ward, Dad." Travis's casual tone was forced. He stood and grabbed a spare chair from an adjacent table for his father, who was using a cane for assistance.

"Manners, son." The older man nodded at Megan.

"Megan, this is my dad, Hugh Jamieson," Travis said reluctantly. "Dad, Megan Merritt."

It was an ideal opportunity to leave, but she was still trying to fathom what was going on.

"Don't get up," Hugh ordered, the same way Travis would have. He shook Megan's hand. His silver-gray hair and weathered countenance didn't detract in the least from his good looks. Quite the opposite—it was clear Travis would still be a very handsome man when he reached his fifties. As Hugh hitched his jeans and sat down, he attracted glances from several "mature" female patrons.

Like Travis, Hugh seemed unaware of the admiration. Yet after he'd hooked his cane over the back of his chair and pushed up the sleeves of his plaid shirt, he unconsciously rubbed his gold wedding band, as if to say, *I'm taken.* What had Travis said? *My wife will have a loyal and faithful husband.*

Why was she thinking about that now? Megan could only attribute it to the confusion he'd thrown her into.

"You're early, Dad." Travis glanced at his watch. "I wasn't expecting you this soon."

"So I see." His father grinned at Megan. "The doc was called away to some emergency, they told me to come back in an hour."

"You want a sandwich? Coffee?" Travis asked. "We have a spare latte." He shifted Megan's cup a couple of inches.

Hugh's lip curled at the prospect. "Your mom packed a lunch for me. A flask of coffee and her home-cured ham sandwiches, better than anything you'll get here. So, Megan, how do you know Travis?" His dark eyes twinkled with interest and something else—could it be relief?

"I work with him," Megan said. "Against him, actually. We're on opposite sides of a divorce case."

"You're handling a divorce, son?" Hugh's eyebrows beetled. Seemed he held the same strong views on marriage as Travis.

"Special case, Dad," Travis said lightly.

She was in this case for the high profile and down-stream revenue opportunity from Theo's business. What made it so special for Travis, since divorce wasn't his thing? The huge fees involved, if Travis was a typical Prescott Palmer lawyer. Except, Megan realized, she'd been thinking he *wasn't* typical. Maybe she should keep reminding herself that he worked for one of the shadiest firms in town. Maybe Robert would remind her of that tonight when he told her whatever he knew about Travis.

Hugh looked at Megan and opened his mouth, but Travis jumped in before he could speak. "Have you thought any more about staying in town for the night, Dad?" He leaned in to allow a woman to squeeze past behind him, her sandwich held over her head.

His father grimaced at the obvious change of subject, but he went with it. "I'll head home, I think. Your mother gets lonesome."

"It's been a whole four hours since he saw Mom," Travis told Megan.

She knew an attempt to manage a conversation when she heard it. She narrowed her eyes.

"That's not to say I can't be tempted. I might have stayed if there was a basketball game on," Hugh conceded.

"Are you a big fan?" Megan reached for her purse,

tucked under her seat. She wouldn't get the truth out of Travis in front of his father. She might as well go back to the office.

"It's my favorite winter sport. Travis gave me a pair of season tickets to the arena for my birthday." Hugh took a drink from his son's water glass. "Nice seats, too. Though not in the same class as the ones you had last week," he said to Travis. He added good-naturedly to Megan, "Travis was given tickets to those fancy executive seats. But right before the game he blew me off for some hot chick."

Hot chick? Me? Megan froze, her purse halfway between the floor and the table. Like her, Travis was in a state of suspended animation, his sandwich hovering near his mouth. Then he shrugged. "Hey, I'm not blind."

Could she have been right with her first, discarded speculation about why he didn't want her dining with Robert? Because he was jealous?

It was preposterous. Yet a deep, female part of her wanted to high-five someone. *Travis thinks I'm hot.* Disconcerted, she dropped her purse back on the floor. She said sympathetically to Hugh, "How rude of him to dump you for a woman."

Still flustered, in a way she never was in a courtroom, she dipped a spoon into the latte she'd spurned, scooped up some whipped cream and ate it. Too sweet, too fatty.

The older man laughed. "It gave me a chance to invite a buddy along in Travis's regular seat, so I didn't mind." He offered a polite smile to an attractive fiftyish woman who'd looked over when he'd laughed. The woman turned back to her companion. "So, Megan, you from a big family?"

"Just my dad and my sisters." She filled him in briefly, concluding with, "Dad's my boss and he doesn't approve of long lunch breaks." It was true. For all Jonah's talk of work-life balance, he was the first to suspect a staff member when they took a proper lunch hour. She pushed her half-eaten wrap away.

"You married? Have kids?" Hugh's eyes rested on her bare ring finger.

"Neither." Megan dug in her wallet for a tip.

Hugh beamed. He was filling in the blanks, and getting it all wrong.

"I'm not in any rush to get married," she said. "And kids aren't in the plan."

"A career woman. Nothing wrong with that." It was so obviously a valiant attempt at fair-mindedness, Megan couldn't help smiling. "So long as your job makes you happy," he added.

Travis cleared his throat. Of course, he knew the job that would make Megan happy was even less likely to include kids, if not marriage. If he thought he could launch into another round of questioning her choices…

"What kind of work do you do, Hugh?" she asked quickly.

"I repair appliances—fridges, dishwashers and the like. On a break at the moment due to this." He patted his hip.

"Does your wife work?" She wedged a couple of dollar bills under the ketchup.

"Like a Trojan. Around the house. Ellie hasn't been out to work since we married. Too busy with me and the kids—Travis is the oldest of four." As if the mention of his wife had triggered a reminder, Hugh pulled his lunch from his jacket pocket. Ignoring the fact he wasn't supposed to bring his own food to a sandwich bar, he spread open the waxed paper. Was that homemade bread? No wonder Travis had inflated ideas of wifely attributes.

"Mom always said it was more important for us to grow up with her around than with a few more luxuries," Travis said pointedly. "That was her idea, by the way. Dad didn't have to chain her to the stove."

"It must have been tough sending kids to college on one income," she said, matching his emphasis. One *low* income, by the sounds of it. "Some women *need* to go out to work." She was one of them, though not for financial reasons.

"Ah, well," Hugh began, "with Travis—"

"We managed," Travis said flatly.

Hugh tucked a paper napkin into the collar of his shirt with deliberate care. "Travis always knew exactly what he wanted," he said.

Money, Megan supposed. If his family had struggled financially, a firm like PPA must have been tempting.

"Dad…" Travis's voice was tight; his fingers curled into his palms. Then he exhaled and straightened them out. "I'm working on it."

"Course you are," Hugh said. "Gina, our baby girl, just started college," he told Megan in a clumsy change of topic. "She's at Duke."

An expensive school. Megan wondered if that was the cause of this moment of tension between father and son. The pregnant silence was beginning to feel like the gap she often sensed between her and her father. The gap between hope and reality.

"I'll bet Gina loves you still calling her a baby." Travis's ribbing sounded forced.

Hugh lifted the top off his sandwich and squeezed mustard onto the ham from the bottle on the table. "Now you mention it, she did flounce into her room and slam the door when she was home on the weekend."

"Gina's eighteen, almost nineteen." Travis's voice softened as he explained the situation to Megan. "But Mom and Dad have trouble remembering she's not a kid."

"She's getting too serious with that boyfriend of hers," Hugh said. "Young guys are only after one thing."

"Like you were when you met Mom?" Travis suggested.

"I was a perfect gentleman toward your mother." The gleam in Hugh's eyes could in no way be described as gentlemanly. "But Gina's boyfriend, that Scott..." He scowled at a piece of ham poking out of his sandwich.

"Don't worry, Dad, I'm sure you raised her right," Travis said. "Besides, you probably still keep that shotgun next to the front door."

Megan snickered, distracted despite herself.

"Seems like only yesterday your mother was changing her poopy diapers," Hugh grumbled.

Megan might have guessed he hadn't done his share of the diaper changing, given Travis's unenlightened attitudes.

"That's something else I'll bet Gina loves hearing," Travis said.

"She's in a sensitive phase." Hugh chomped into his bread.

It was so clear that both men adored Gina, despite

her apparently dubious taste in men, Megan felt a shameful pang of envy for this teenager she'd never met.

"Your mother's hoping Gina will come home for the Christmas party this weekend," Hugh said. "She's going to that boy's family for Thanksgiving, but hopefully we'll see her Saturday. Your mom tells me we won't see you for turkey."

"Sorry, Dad. Kyle's taking the anniversary of his parents' death worse than usual. I told him I'd spend the holiday with him and his sister."

"Anyway, maybe you can talk some sense into Gina on the weekend, you've always had a handle on her."

"Sure," Travis agreed. His sister must be sixteen or seventeen years younger than he was. No doubt he'd acquired some of his aptitude for children from living with her.

"Looks like we'll have a decent crowd at the social," Hugh said. "Maybe even the Laings. Might be the perfect time to spread some good news." His encouraging smile at Travis wasn't returned. The silence was back.

"Dad, Megan has to leave." Travis pushed his chair away from the table and stood. "Would you like me to ask for a doggy bag?" He indicated the remains of her wrap.

"No, thanks," she said, annoyed, as she shook hands with Hugh. She did need to go, but that wasn't for him to say. "I have a date tonight, I'll save my appetite."

Travis's mouth tightened. "Don't forget, you owe me a Christmas party invitation."

His stupid bet over his stupid coffee theory. She'd had it up to here with his insistence on analyzing her.

The last thing she needed was him sharing his hare-brained ideas with her father at the Christmas party. She ignored that he'd been right and said loftily, "I never gamble."

CHAPTER SEVEN

A VAGUE MEMORY of wandering hands from her last date with Robert Grayson made Megan dress even more conservatively than usual that evening. Her black jersey dress might be formfitting, but it had a high neck, long sleeves, and ended modestly just above her knee.

She applied more makeup than usual, so all that black wouldn't wash her out, and decided the result was good enough for Robert.

He arrived at Salt just as she did, on time at seven. His greeting was a respectful kiss on the cheek. Then he lessened the courteous effect by purring, "Verrry nice," as he inspected her outfit.

They were seated in one of the holly-trimmed booths on the left-hand side of the spacious room, which required passing the table where Megan and Travis had sat last time. Tonight an older couple occupied it, sharing a slice of cheesecake.

"So, Megan, with any luck we might be working together soon," Robert said after they'd ordered.

Not if I can help it. "Uh-huh." She swirled her glass, watched the wine churn.

"I hear you've done a great job of building up the family practice," he said.

"It's the fastest growing area of the firm."

"I think our friendship would stand us in good stead, were we to become colleagues," he continued. "I wouldn't see ours as a boss-employee relationship."

She sipped her wine. "Considering we'd both be partners in the firm, I'd be surprised if you did." Had Robert always been this pompous? *Or am I getting spoiled by a man who doesn't take anything seriously, who flirts like a sailor on shore leave?*

Appalled at the thought, she summoned some enthusiasm for her companion. They talked recent cases, industry gossip. When Robert had drained his first glass of wine and the waiter had poured him a second, Megan maneuvered the conversation back to the managing partner's job at Merritt, Merritt & Finch.

"For Dad to put you on the short list means he has a high opinion of you." Personally, she wondered why Robert was so dense that he hadn't picked up on what Travis had taken five minutes to figure out. That she wanted the job herself.

Robert preened. "Jonah expressed some concerns about the way the criminal division has been run since Cynthia left. He thinks I might have the firm hand necessary to pull it back into line."

Firm hand in criminal, Megan noted. "What sort of profit targets do you think we should be aiming for in that area?" She sat back as the waiter delivered their appetizers: pumpkin soup for her, chicken liver paté for Robert. She picked up her spoon and sampled the soup. Creamy, velvet-smooth, with a delicate hint of nutmeg.

"In my view," Robert said, "you can't expect the same return in criminal that you can in family, even though in criminal the cases are…"

The rest of his words flew over her head as, out of the corner of her eye, Megan caught a familiar shape, a familiar way of moving. At the center table she thought of as hers and Travis's.

It couldn't be…she inched discreetly across so she could see beyond the booth.

It is.

The older couple had left, and Travis was settling a pretty brunette into the chair facing the door. Megan's seat.

She choked on the pumpkin soup.

"Are you okay?" Robert topped up her water glass and glanced around, presumably in search of someone to perform the Heimlich maneuver.

"Fine," Megan croaked. She took a long slug of her water. When she put the glass down, she glanced back at Travis. He'd taken the same seat as last time, facing the extravagantly decorated Christmas tree at the far end of the room, and was looking right at her. He lifted his wineglass in a toast.

"As I was saying," Robert went on, "you tend to find that margins in a family law division…"

Dammit, she lost him again. Though she managed to keep her eyes on Robert, her awareness was lured to Travis like an ant to honey. How dare he show up, knowing she'd be here?

Maybe he *was* jealous? She edged along the booth so she wouldn't have to crane, and found Travis engrossed in conversation with his date. He laughed at something the woman said and leaned in closer.

So much for the jealousy theory. To her irritation, Megan found herself angling toward Robert, too. It was the encouragement he'd been waiting for. His voice dropped half an octave, as if his talk of margins and billable hours could be remotely construed as sexy. He was a good-looking guy, but all getting up close did for Megan was show her she had a strong preference for darker eyes, lit with teasing humor.

Robert was telling her about what changes he would make at Merritt, Merritt & Finch. Important information she should absorb if she wanted to beat him to her father's job…and yet every single word was chased out of her mind by a plague of questions about Travis's motives.

By the time Robert's dessert arrived, Megan was ready to throw in the towel and leave. A marked contrast with when she'd dined here with Travis…they'd both ordered dessert and coffee, neither of them in any hurry to end the night. Robert's foot touched hers under the table, jerking her back to the moment. When she retracted her foot, his slid forward, and this time his calf rested against her leg. A sharp kick might give him the hint.

"You're great company, Megan," he said.

Kicking him seemed a churlish reaction to the compliment. "Thanks," she replied without enthusiasm

"I've often thought it a shame you and I didn't make a better go of dating," he mused. "There are a lot of what I'd call power couples in our industry. Husband-and-wife legal teams. It makes sense."

"It sounds…unnerving." She thought about the way Travis always seemed to read her mind.

"Your own parents," he pointed out. "The way my dad tells it, your mother was an excellent attorney."

"My parents divorced," she reminded him.

"Always a risk." His knee nudged hers. "But with the right prenup, one can keep things amicable."

"Prenups are unromantic." She agreed with Robert, so why was she spouting Travis's outdated view?

"Hello, Megan." The man himself arrived alongside their booth, his girlfriend with him. Travis glanced down beneath the table.

"Oh, hi." As if she hadn't quite registered his presence before now. She allowed Robert's leg to stay where it was. If she was going to kick anyone, she'd rather make it Travis. "You remember Robert Grayson?"

The two men shook hands. Travis introduced them to his date, Allie Fleming.

"Nice to meet you," she told Megan. Her hair was more chestnut than brown, a rich color that gleamed in the restaurant lighting. When she smiled, her eyes lit up. She looked relaxed, happy and…nice, dammit.

"Do you work with Travis, Allie?" she asked, to fill the silence.

"I work from home," the woman said. "I have a business baking cookies, which I sell to cafés." Well, wasn't she just perfect? Beautiful and she made a living out of the kind of *homemaking* skills Travis admired.

"Best cookies you ever tasted." Travis's hand brushed Allie's shoulder.

"He's so sweet," the woman said to Megan.

"You think?" she asked, before she could curb the impulse.

Travis snorted, but Allie's expression cooled at the insult to her date, whose eyes, Megan noticed, had once again drifted downward.

"You two having a nice evening?" Travis asked.

"Wonderful." Megan sent Robert the kind of dazzling smile her sister Sabrina made a career of. To her gratification, he did look dazzled.

"We need to go," Travis said abruptly.

Allie smiled up at him. "Yeah, I need an early night."

How interesting. Megan didn't want to analyze the acid burn in the pit of her stomach.

After Travis left, the restaurant seemed dimmer, the ambience less stimulating.

"Is there anything you should tell me about Travis?" she asked Robert. Right now, she would welcome the news that he'd murdered two wives and chopped up their bodies with a chain saw, she was so desperate to kill her awareness of him.

Robert tensed. "What did Jamieson say?"

"Nothing, I just sensed a problem."

"I don't like the guy," he said. "I don't like his firm's ethics."

She could hardly argue with that.

She wanted to scream when Robert ordered coffee and cognac, unfazed by her pointed refusal of another drink and her glance at her watch. Now that he had Megan's foot locked between his, he wasn't about to let go.

It was eleven o'clock by the time he paid the check—Megan was too annoyed to even consider splitting it—and she escaped.

Outside, clouds obscured the moon and the only light source was the orange streetlight in the parking lot.

"Are you okay to drive?" she asked as they neared her car. Robert had drunk more than she had, but he seemed steady enough. She hoped desperately she wouldn't have to offer him a ride home.

He bumped against the Jeep next to her BMW. When he straightened, he was much closer, confining her in the space between the two cars. "I'm fine. I had a great night, Megan."

"Me, too." It wasn't as if she was on the witness stand, under oath. She pressed the button to unlock her car. "Well, good—umph."

Robert had her locked in his arms, his mouth mashed against hers.

It all came back to her now, the way his kisses had left her cold those few times they'd dated. This one rated slightly worse than neutral on the kissing scale, thanks to the alcohol fumes.

At first, Megan concentrated on keeping her lips pressed firmly together against the probing of his tongue. Since she might have encouraged him to think she would welcome his advances, she would give him five seconds of courtesy time. Five...four...three...two...one. *Ding*.

She managed to twist her head aside. "Okay, it's getting—" Erk! Talking had given him the chance to slip his tongue into her mouth. No, she definitely did not rate him as a kisser. No finesse whatsoever. She yanked away and gave him a shove. "That's enough. Good *night*, Robert."

He got the message and pulled back, his hands still at her waist. His voice was sulky. "Can I help it if you're so—"

"Out of your league," snarled a male voice behind him.

"Travis!" Megan stumbled against her car as Travis grabbed Robert by the neck and hauled him away.

"Beat it, Grayson," he said. "Or you'll have more trouble than you bargained for." He released Robert with a flick of the hand reminiscent of tossing something in the trash.

The gesture wasn't wasted on Robert. "You lay another finger on me, and you'll be in court on an assault charge," he barked.

Travis didn't back down, and the two men eyed each other. They were the same height, but even in their dinner clothes Travis's toned fitness made Robert look soft.

"Travis, you're overreacting," Megan said. "Stop it, both of you."

Robert straightened his jacket, buttoned it as if he were in no particular hurry. "Good night, Megan," he said. Then walked away with a speed that suggested he wasn't impervious to Travis's threat.

"What were you doing letting a jerk like that within ten feet of you?" Travis demanded, as soon as Robert had climbed into his Lexus.

"I'll have dinner with whoever I like." Megan patted down her hair. "How come you're still here? You left nearly an hour ago." Not that she'd been counting. She scanned the parking lot for Allie, but there was no sign of the woman.

"I saw your car here and I wanted to make sure you got away from Grayson okay." Travis scrutinized her face, checking for who knows what. "I came back."

"You shouldn't have bothered. I'm fed up with you butting into my personal life." She jabbed a finger at his chest through his black shirt. She whipped it away again. "I'll date Robert every night of the week if I want to."

"You will not."

She clutched her head. "Travis…"

Another couple exited the restaurant and glanced curiously in the direction of their raised voices.

"Dammit, Megan," Travis muttered. "I shouldn't tell you this, but Grayson was questioned by the police about a date rape allegation a couple of years back."

She reeled backward. "I don't believe you. I would have heard."

"He paid hush money. Seems he wasn't willing to put attorney-client confidentiality to the test in his own firm. He schlepped across town to PPA—that kind of transaction is right up our alley," Travis said grimly. "The money was paid out to the woman without admission of guilt."

"So…no prosecution."

"And a guarantee of confidentiality," he said.

"Do—do you think it was true? What she accused him of?" Megan shuddered at the memory of Robert's tongue, invading her mouth.

"He's innocent until proved guilty, so it doesn't matter what I think. But it does matter to me that you don't go out with him." He reached over to tuck a strand of hair behind her ear.

"I—I thought Robert had some dirt on you, and that's why you didn't want me to go." All this time, he'd been genuinely worried about her. Not trying to steal her client. Guilty, she took a step toward him. Her foot brushed something; she glanced down and saw her purse—she must have dropped it while Robert was groping her.

Travis picked it up, dusting it off. Satisfied, he handed it to her. "Are you willing to believe a PPA lawyer over one of the pillars of the legal fraternity?"

Megan searched Travis's eyes in the orange glow of the streetlight. "Yes. But why didn't you tell me earlier?"

"I told you not to go out with him."

"And you thought I should *obey* you?" She paused,

then went fishing. "Save that macho stuff for Allie. If she's still talking to you after you abandoned her." She tried to sound disapproving.

"Allie understood. She's an old friend."

Ex-girlfriend, she thought.

"We never dated," Travis said.

Megan tamped down a surge of elation. She fingered her keys but didn't move toward her car. "I'm really not interested in your love life."

His laugh was slow-drifting, like fog on the evening air. "Your curiosity is written all over your face."

Not possible. She was known for her aloofness, her inscrutability.

"If I'm curious, it's about why you took your *friend* home, then came back here to protect me." She gripped the strap of her purse. "Do you do the same for every woman Robert dates? Or just me?"

"Just you." His voice was low. He sighed. "Hell, you're right. This is none of my business. You can take care of yourself."

Suddenly, Megan didn't want to. "Then why are you here?"

He tipped his head back, scanned the skies as if the answer might be there. "Damned if I know."

A spurt of laughter escaped her. Then she said with courtroom objectivity, "It looks a lot like jealousy."

"It does, doesn't it?" He sounded surprised. "I've never been jealous before."

"Must be something else then," she said practically.

He gave her a brooding look. "Do me a favor. Don't date Grayson again."

As if she would. Still, best not to capitulate too easily. "Pushing your luck, Travis, telling me what to do."

"I like to live dangerously." A spark arced between them, invisible but electric.

"Despite appearances," she said, "tonight wasn't a date. It was meant to be a business dinner."

His gaze traveled down her short, figure-hugging black dress. "I suppose you wore that because you think it's modest."

"It is." Though from the sudden glint in his eyes, Megan wasn't so sure. She put a hand to her throat, where the high collar of her dress ended.

"I have news for you." He touched the same spot, the brush of his finger a light caress against her neck. "This is the kind of dress, you put an incredible figure like yours in it, and it drives a man wild." He sounded intriguingly husky.

Megan would admit her figure was one of her best assets, but *incredible*...? She was fairly sure that would cop a misrepresentation rap in court.

"Well, look at that." He closed the gap between them and bared his teeth in a dangerous grin. Megan tingled all over. "I just realized," he said, "we're in the exact same spot we were in for our first kiss."

Tingling turned to a heat that spread inward. She managed to say coolly, "That wasn't a real kiss."

"Aw, shucks, Ms. Megan, that was one of my better efforts."

"Are you ever serious?" she demanded.

He put one hand on either side of her on her car, effectively pinning her there. "I've been nothing but serious where you're concerned, Megan, from the moment we met. I've never known anyone like you."

Did he have any idea how seductive that was to a woman who'd always existed in the shadow of more talented, more beautiful sisters? "Cynthia is smarter," she began, unable to prevent herself repeating the conditioning of her childhood.

"I doubt that," Travis said. "And I don't care. I like *you*."

Her heart stopped in her chest, then resumed pounding so loudly she thought he must hear it. "That doesn't make sense, given our differences."

"No doubt you can think of a more logical explanation."

She didn't want to, but it was probably best that she did. "It could be your overprotective chauvinistic streak kicking in."

"In which case, the simplest thing," he guessed, "would be for you to thank me for dispatching Robert, get in your car, drive home and not have to worry about complications."

"Exactly." Disappointment warred with relief. Relief won. "Thank you for dispatching Robert."

He remained silent, until she met his eyes, dark as midnight. "I hoped you might thank me in the traditional fashion," he said.

She swallowed. "You want me to write you a note?"

In reply, he tilted her chin with one finger. All of her body heat converged on that point, making her feverish.

"Travis, I don't think—" She fought for coherence. "It's been a long, complicated night, and I'm all kissed out."

"Don't worry, we'll keep it simple." His finger moved up to caress the seam of her lips. "Mmm," he murmured, the sound slow and deep, as if she was as beautiful as Sabrina.

How was she supposed to resist?

Her thoughts must be all over her face again, because Travis smiled—an intimate, sensuous smile—then he touched his lips to hers. Not for much longer than that first, accidental kiss. Entirely the opposite of Robert's unwelcome advance. When he pulled away, Megan felt…cheated.

"Is that it?" she asked.

"No, Megs," he said roughly, "that is not it."

He kissed her again, and this time…this time…it was magic. His mouth fit perfectly against hers, firm, seeking, sensual. He nipped her lower lip and desire shot through Megan, the secret code that opened her mouth. His tongue slipped in, flicked against hers, then began a slow mating as tormenting as it was satisfying.

Megan twined her arms around his neck, pressed closer. He groaned and muttered, "This is impossible," even as he traced the line of her jaw with whisper-light kisses. His hands moved to cup her bottom.

The hint of a night breeze passed between them, cooling Megan's heated skin. Blowing reality over her.

"Travis, stop." It came out barely louder than a whisper, rather than the command she'd intended, yet he immediately released her. So fast, she tripped against her car. He grabbed her to steady her, but this time his touch was impersonal. "Are you okay?" he asked.

Was he referring to her stumble, or the kiss?

"I'm fine." She opened the car and tossed her purse over to the passenger seat, using the distraction to reclaim her breath. And her sense.

At midnight, the craziest things could seem logical, inevitable. She rubbed her eyes—uh-oh, all that mascara had to go somewhere—suddenly desperate to be in her own bed. Alone. "I'd better leave. We have a big meeting with the Hoskinses tomorrow."

The moonlight magic would be gone, and the stark light of day would be filled with Theo and Barbara, their bickering, Megan's worries about her job. Tomorrow, Travis would be the enemy.

He looked at her for a long moment, his expression unreadable. Then he laughed softly. "Always on the case, aren't you, Megs?"

He held her car door open. Megan climbed in, keeping her focus on the windshield, then the seat belt, then the ignition, then the gear shift. Her door snicked closed. She drove straight out, without looking back.

What a bizarre night. She'd gone to dinner with her mind set on industrial espionage against Robert. She'd ended the evening mindless, in Travis's arms.

Mindless was bad. Mindless wouldn't get her what she wanted, which wasn't the casual kisses of a semi-reputable lawyer. If she wanted to win her father over, she needed to engage her brain and disengage her... other parts.

CHAPTER EIGHT

TRAVIS WASN'T normally prone to recriminations over something as insubstantial as a kiss, but at least a dozen times on Tuesday he was assailed by regrets over the previous night's combustible encounter with Megan.

He'd never meant for it to happen, had returned to the restaurant after dropping Allie at home purely with the intention of making sure Megan got away from Robert safely.

Kissing her was definitely not in the plan.

The plan was to use the Hoskins case to get close to Jonah Merritt, not to his daughter.

But as so often happened when Megan was around, he could no more have resisted her than he could have stopped breathing.

Which didn't say much about his ability to learn from his mistakes. Ten years ago, he'd made an error in judgment, let a bunch of people down by joining PPA, no matter that his reasons had been noble. Now, just as he had a chance to fix his career mistake, he risked sabotaging his plans for personal happiness.

Kissing Megan was too damn distracting. A guy could forget his determination to settle down and start a family, and instead succumb to honey-haired temptation.

No more, he vowed, as he and Barbara Hoskins took the elevator to the third floor of Merritt, Merritt & Finch's building for Wednesday afternoon's division of assets meeting, dedicated to the Hoskinses' extremely valuable share portfolio.

Megan had obviously decided retreat was the best course of action, too. She greeted him with distant formality before she and Theo sat down on the other side of the imposing, carved-leg table.

For the next three hours, Barbara and Theo bickered and quibbled over every last penny of their stock portfolio until the air was heavy with acrimony.

"I should keep the Mirror Corp shares," Theo said, just as Travis was contemplating breaking a window to let in some oxygen. It was past five o'clock, almost dark outside. "You said they were a waste of money when I bought them."

"The same day you bought Enron, wasn't it?" Barbara sneered. "I want half of Mirror Corp."

The couple were supposed to let their lawyers do the negotiating, but they couldn't resist sniping.

"My client is willing to accede in the matter of the Mirror Corp shares," Megan told Travis in a rare pause in the arguing, "so long as your client agrees to an equal division of the Forest Products options."

"I earned those options working eighteen hour days at that company," Barbara sputtered.

Travis wondered who'd looked after the kids while she worked those long days. But Barbara was his client, so he was on her side. At least she wasn't an alcoholic, like the kids' dad.

"Your client can have thirty percent of Forest Products," he said. "No more."

Megan's gaze clashed with his; then she looked down at her notes. "We'll take it," she said, and he wondered if he'd given her more than she expected.

They wrapped up at five-thirty, by which time Travis was ready to gag his client and punch Megan's. He didn't know how Megan handled divorces all the time. It was enough to turn anyone off marriage.

Barbara left in a hurry to do some Christmas shopping, while Theo went to relieve the babysitter at the family home until Barbara returned.

While Travis checked his notes against those made by Trisha, Megan's paralegal, Megan didn't hide her attempt to observe over Trisha's shoulder. Did she think he'd try to sneak a few alterations in under her radar?

Last night, he'd thought she trusted him.

Unconsciously, she fiddled with a button on her suit jacket as she monitored Trisha. Her fingers slid over the polished silver disc, then circled the rim. He remembered her hands in his hair, her body against his during that electrifying kiss outside Salt. He hauled his brain back into line, just as the meeting room door opened.

"Megan," Jonah Merritt said.

Her head snapped around. "Dad?"

He was here, the man Travis was beginning to wonder if he'd sold his soul to meet.

Jonah's complexion looked better than it had that day in The Jury Room, but his eyes were slightly sunken.

"I'm on my way to have a drink with Judge Pearson, I thought I'd call in," Jonah said to his daughter. He nodded at Trisha, who was leaving the room, and directed a politely inquiring glance at Travis.

Travis propelled himself to his feet. He stuck out a

hand and leaned across the table. "Mr. Merritt, I'm Travis Jamieson."

Jonah was a couple of inches shorter than Travis, but his sheer presence meant he took over a room. Or a courtroom. His handshake was firm to the point of punishing, his scrutiny piercing. He might not have taken any of Travis's calls, but from the pursing of his lips he knew who Travis was.

"You're Barbara Hoskins's lawyer." His tone said he was aware Travis was more than that.

"That's right." He returned Jonah's scrutiny measure for measure.

Megan bustled to kiss her father's cheek. "Dad, you're supposed to stay away from the office."

"It's only a quick visit." Jonah pulled out a chair and sank into it. He scanned the room with proprietary satisfaction. "It's still my firm, despite what the doctors say."

Megan's gaze softened. "Of course it's still your firm." She clipped a plastic sleeve of receipts into a binder and sat, too. "Travis and I *were* just going over the points we agreed upon in our meeting." The emphasis on *were* and the pointed look she gave Travis told him he could leave.

Travis wasn't going anywhere. Not when this was the first and only opportunity he'd had to connect with Jonah. He suspected she wouldn't issue a more direct instruction because she couldn't trust him to fall into line. She wouldn't want to show weakness in front of her dad. He sat down again, ignored the tightening of her lips.

"Let's go grab a coffee," she suggested to Jonah. "Then we can go to my office and I'll give you an update on the Hoskins case." Effectively removing Travis from the scene.

"No point drinking coffee without caffeine," Jonah grumbled. He pointed to Megan's file. "May I?" Without waiting for permission, he pulled it toward him and began to read her notes.

"As you can see, we're close to a resolution on division of assets," she said. Travis would have said *close* was an exaggeration. "The real battles will be custody and Mrs. Hoskins's challenge to the prenup."

Hardened court warrior that he was, Jonah's eyes lit up at the mention of a battle. "What are the grounds for the prenup challenge?"

Travis had supplied Megan with a list of his client's objections to the prenuptial agreement as part of their preliminary paperwork. They hadn't got to discussing it yet, but he was a hundred percent ready. He jumped in. "The agreement was signed just five days before the wedding. Mrs. Hoskins asserts there was an element of coercion."

Megan scowled at him. "The contract was drafted well in advance, Mrs. Hoskins had plenty of time to read it. She didn't sign earlier because she was traveling on business."

"Then there's the matter of actively appreciating assets," Travis said. "Mrs. Hoskins's financial expertise greatly augmented the value of the preexisting share portfolio defined in the prenup as Mr. Hoskins's separate property."

"It's Mrs. Hoskins's *opinion* that she can take some credit for that." Megan's knuckles turned white on her pencil; she looked as if she was contemplating using it as a deadly weapon. Jonah, on the other hand, clearly relished being in the middle of the debate. He stretched his arms out and laced his fingers as he nodded. There was no mistaking his fondness for Megan...nor his interest in Travis.

"Travis knows his client is on shaky ground," Megan continued. "Somewhere in there—" she nodded at Travis's briefcase "—he has our memorandum pointing out that Barbara didn't disclose all her assets before the marriage."

Travis decided getting bogged down in who owned what wasn't the way to impress Jonah. "There's some precedent to suggest my client has a strong case," he said, and widened the discussion to include comparisons with a couple of other divorces, and some commentary on current trends in judges' decisions about prenup enforcement. Nothing Megan wouldn't already know, of course. But he had a few examples up his sleeve he hoped would surprise her in court.

Jonah kicked back in his seat and clasped his hands behind his head. "Sounds like you might have your work cut out defending Theo's position," he commented to Megan. She stiffened, but before she could reply, her father asked Travis a couple of insightful questions. Nothing that would require disclosure of client-confidential material—Jonah was the consummate professional—just the kind of questions that made Travis think hard to justify his opinions. He could learn a lot from this man.

Travis observed how Megan hung on Jonah's words, how she would reach toward him, sometimes touching his sleeve, sometimes pulling back. When it came to her dad, she had a bad case of hero worship. Not that it showed through in her voice; she sounded calm and competent and professional. Only someone as tuned into her as Travis unwillingly was would pick up that she was throwing her all into the discussion and getting increasingly panicked that it might not be enough.

Enough, presumably, for her father to recognize her potential as a future leader of the firm.

Travis felt for her. It must be frustrating to be pigeon-holed as being at the limit of your capabilities. He had the opposite problem. His parents never doubted he could do anything, which left him scrambling to explain why he wasn't living the life he'd always said he wanted.

"I hear Atkins screwed up the cross in the O'Shea trial today," Jonah said grimly, changing the subject. Like most of Atlanta, Travis had a working knowledge of the homicide case that was hogging the headlines. Atkins was the Merritt, Merritt & Finch partner leading the defense team. In a case like this, based on circum-stantial evidence, a solid cross-examination to discredit the witnesses was crucial.

"I thought your people would Plan B the guy," Travis said. "There was plenty of opportunity to cast the blame on someone else."

Jonah removed his glasses and began polishing them. "Have you done any criminal work, Jamieson?"

Travis shook his head. "I hold a management role at PPA, which requires me to understand the criminal side." Which Jonah would know if he'd bothered to read Travis's résumé. "But I'm no match for a good criminal attorney."

Jonah sighed. "Times like this I wish Cynthia wasn't such a highflier. If she was here the case wouldn't be in this mess. But when that girl gets an ambition in her sights, there's no stopping her."

"I have ambition, too, Dad." Megan seemed to speak without thinking, an automatic response.

"You're doing a great job running the family division," Jonah assured her. "Our new managing partner will be playing catch-up until he gets to know the place as well as you do." His expression became wistful. "If Cynthia was here it would be blessedly simple. She's an amazing lawyer, a gifted manager…."

"Since I know more about this place than anyone," Megan said, "maybe you should—"

"We've talked about this." Jonah glanced sharply at Travis. "You know where I stand."

She subsided, but her eyes glittered. She was hurt. Dammit, the protective instincts that had sent Travis back to the restaurant so he could drag Robert Grayson off her returned in full force.

With difficulty, he held himself rigid. It would be pure madness to hurl himself across the table and give Jonah a severe shaking for his lack of faith in his daughter.

Then he heard himself say, "Sounds like Cynthia's just about as good a lawyer as Megan." *Shut up.*

Jonah and Megan swiveled toward him, mouths identically agape as if he'd launched into a tap dance right here in their meeting room.

He was glad he'd stood up for Megan. No matter what people thought in Jackson Creek, no matter what his family feared, he hadn't gone over to the dark side.

"Megan's an excellent lawyer, and extremely hard-working," Jonah agreed stiffly. The corners of his mouth relaxed as he regarded his daughter. "You have rings around your eyes the size of saucers, my dear."

Travis stifled a smile that would smack of condescension. Megan might look tired, but she could handle her job. Two jobs, probably.

"Not a problem, Dad."

"No point damaging your health," Jonah admonished her. "What are you doing besides work?"

Megan flipped over the sleeves in her ring binder, apparently engrossed in the search for some document. Her cheeks were pink. "I had a date last night."

Grayson. Travis's fingers itched to slug the guy all over again.

"And I, um, I'm going to Six Flags tomorrow evening." She stared at Travis, defying him to tell her dad the truth. That the amusement park outing was another counseling session with the Hoskins family.

"There's a young man," her father announced, "Nick Stanton, Wally Stanton's son. He's just back from a couple of years overseas, and needs someone to bring him up to date with the Atlanta legal system. I told his father you'll meet up with him. Maybe dinner."

"I don't need you arranging my dates," Megan protested. She ducked her head, so Travis couldn't see her face.

"He's a decent fellow," Jonah said. "Do it for me."

Ah, that old standby, emotional blackmail. Always more effective when the recipient is insecure in the blackmailer's affections. Travis shifted in his seat.

"I'll consider it." Megan's glower warned Travis not to butt in. Yeah, well, he had no intention of interfering if she wanted to date Nick Stanton. It had been a long time since Travis had hung out with him, but he knew for sure that the guy was no jerk she needed saving from, like Robert Grayson.

He was Megan's perfect match.

Through the rushing sound in his head, Travis became aware of Jonah dusting his hands together. "Good girl."

Travis waited for Megan to blow up at her dad the way she would at him if he tried a line like that. But she settled for a taut smile.

"Maybe you should hold off until you're done with the Hoskins case, though," Jonah suggested. "You'll need your wits about you if you want to do your best for Theo."

Megan's shoulders were rigid with humiliation.

"Mr. Merritt—" the words slipped out of Travis before he consciously articulated them "—don't you think that as a senior partner Megan has a handle on how to run a case by now?"

Megan started; her pencil went rolling across the table.

"Excuse me?" Jonah said.

Travis couldn't back down now. "I was under the impression Megan hasn't lost a custody case in five years." A statistic he would do well to remember.

Jonah drummed his fingers on the table. "Doesn't mean she might not make a mistake."

"Excuse me, I'm right here," Megan said.

"Most likely it *does* mean that," Travis replied. "My father believes his kids need support and encouragement, not doubt and undermining."

Megan made an inarticulate sound.

"And your father would be?" Jonah demanded.

"Just a regular guy with a lot of faith in his kids to live the way he raised them." Which was why Travis was mired in guilt right now, the whole reason he was after this damned job. "My dad's the man I respect most in this world."

Jonah's finger-drumming grew more agitated. Travis gathered from Megan's fascination with the movement that this wasn't a good sign.

"You have a nerve walking into my company and telling me how to talk to my daughter."

"I tell it like I see it," Travis returned.

"You won't be doing that again," Jonah said, with a significance that bypassed Megan but made Travis's heart sink.

He'd just talked himself out of a job.

Jonah stood up and held on to the back of his chair, breathing heavily. Great, had Travis just given him another coronary? "I worry about you, Megan," Jonah said. "I'm not trying to undermine you—I know you're as smart as anyone."

"Thanks, Dad." She kissed his cheek.

Travis might as well not have bothered sticking up for her. Well, wasn't this peachy, he thought, as Jonah left without saying goodbye to him. Father and daughter relations were mended, and meanwhile, he'd just blown whatever slim chance he'd had of impressing Jonah Merritt and getting the job that would restore his own father's pride in him.

CHAPTER NINE

AFTER SHE SAW her father to the elevator, Megan walked back to the meeting room on leaden feet. Despite the crumb of comfort her father had tossed her, she was as far away as ever from convincing Dad to give her a chance.

Despite Travis's defense of her.

She paused in the doorway. Travis had his elbows on the table, his head in his hands. He looked like she felt. That didn't make sense.

"I appreciate your attempt to help," she said awkwardly.

He glanced up. "No problem."

She advanced to the table. "Dad doesn't like being told he's wrong."

"Doesn't mean you should let him get away with undervaluing you."

She snapped her binder closed. "I don't need your advice."

"As always, your need to put me in my place outweighs your gratitude. Lucky I enjoy it."

He stretched, and she caught the ripple of muscle beneath his shirt. She'd managed to go through the meeting with Travis without thinking about last night. The humming of her pulse told her the statute of limitations was up. "That suggests your life has singularly little fun in it," she said. "You surprise me."

Just like that, the atmosphere shifted, lightened.

"You really do think I'm out dating every night, don't you?" Travis's voice was low and taunting.

"I don't actually think about you all that much," she said apologetically.

"Liar." He bounced to his feet. "You know what we both need?"

Her whole body tingled. *Not that.* "A time-out from each other?"

He walked to the window; she wondered if he would glimpse her father walking away. "A relaxing dinner. This has been a hell of a day."

"*I* need to go to bed," she said. And realized her mistake.

"If you insist," he said generously. "But I'd rather we ate first. Purely for stamina reasons."

"Alone," she managed to say, over the bombardment of images—heated flesh, tangled limbs, hungry mouths—his words provoked.

"If you go home now, you won't get to sleep," he said. "Your mind will be racing all night."

"Maybe," she conceded, when there was no maybe about it.

"There's this place I know, it's relaxing, with home-style cooking."

It sounded like bliss. "I guess I do have to eat."

"I'll drive." He dangled his keys from one finger. "No point both of us fighting the rush-hour traffic."

She hesitated. She almost never let a guy drive her on a date. *This isn't a date, it's a business dinner.*

Probably. She rolled her shoulders. "Okay, but only because I'm tired enough to fall asleep at the wheel."

He grinned, with a flash of his usual energy. "That's what I like, to be the choice of last resort."

"I'm sure you're used to it," she said affably.

He laughed. Something about Travis's laugh always made the stresses of her job fade into, if not insignificance, something much more manageable.

Megan fastened her seat belt as they left the underground parking lot. "Where are we going?"

"My place."

She grabbed the door handle. "No way."

He put a hand on her knee, anchoring her. "I do a mean steak, and it's easier to relax at home than in a restaurant. We're not going far, I'm in Virginia Highlands."

"Travis, this isn't a good idea. We're colleagues."

"It's the best idea I've had all day," he said. He flipped his turn signal and moved into the left-hand lane. "Call it a pity meal."

"I'll bet your life is full of those," she muttered. *Not.*

Virginia Highlands, with its mix of cute cottages and more expensive homes, and one-off stores, was Megan's favorite part of town.

Travis's street was in the process of gentrification, some homes renovated and some in what Realtors liked to call original condition. Travis's two-story cottage was somewhere in between, he told her as he opened the front door. "It still needs work, but you'll get the idea."

He switched on the hallway light, illuminating polished wooden floors scattered with colorful, modern rugs. Megan followed him into the living room, where floor-to-ceiling bookshelves lined one wall. On the other wall, above the fireplace, hung a painting—she recognized it as one by Dawn Rodriguez, a local artist.

"This place is so cozy," she said.

"You think anyone who works at PPA must be a slob?" He crouched in front of the fire, set a match to the kindling in the grate.

"Just wondering why you need a homemaker wife, when you seem to have talents in that direction yourself."

"I only do the macho stuff, the things that need power tools. My wife will have to be the cook." He slid her purse from her shoulder and tossed it onto the couch. "The rest of the place isn't so civilized. It's taking me longer than I wanted. I need to get more time off work."

"Any more time off work and you'll be a renovator moonlighting as a lawyer." She perused the bookshelves and found a collection far more eclectic than her own.

"You should try this." He pulled a book down for her. *Silence in the Tomb*. The book he'd been reading that day outside her office. "It's good," he said. "Give it a try."

"I don't have time to read." But she stuck it in her handbag just to be polite.

In the corner, stood a Christmas tree, a real pine, with haphazard decorations: a snowman here, an angel there, a few stars. "You overpaid your decorator." Megan plucked a pine needle and ran it beneath her nose, inhaling the forest scent.

"Those are my own efforts you're knocking." Travis clapped a hand to his chest. "After all of those Martha Stewart videos I watched."

"Let me guess, she's your pinup girl."

He relieved her of her jacket, taking in the fitted lilac silk blouse over her slim skirt. "I wouldn't say that."

"But Martha's such a homemaker."

"You seem to think I'm entirely one-dimensional."

"Aren't you?"

His eyes went to her lips. "I definitely have at least two dimensions."

"Let's go cook," Megan said quickly.

The kitchen hadn't been updated in maybe fifty years, apart from the state-of-the-art oven and dish-washer and a coffee machine that might have been lifted from NASA. Travis pulled a pack of steak from the fridge. "Do you want to be head chef or sous-chef?" He threw her a black calico apron from a hook on the wall.

She tied the apron around her waist, saw the flare of interest in his eyes. "Don't get excited," she warned. "I don't cook."

"I guess that means I'm head chef."

She rose to the challenge. "I'm sure I could manage steak."

"A common misconception. Most people can't cook steak to save themselves. You can be on chopping."

"Why does that sound less important than whatever you're going to do?"

He grinned. "Ease up on the global domination ambition, Megs, just for a couple of hours." He rummaged in the fridge and passed her basil, garlic and—

"Anchovies?" She turned the jar in her hand. The tiny fish were packed in oil that had turned thick and cloudy in the fridge.

"We're making a green salsa."

"Doesn't that come in jars at the supermarket?"

He made a cross with his fingers, a warding-off-evil sign.

Travis cooked as he did everything else, with an easy, relaxed mastery. After Megan finished chopping the salsa ingredients, she was promoted, as he put it, to topping and tailing the green beans.

She squinted at him as he brushed olive oil over the steaks. "I thought you'd consider this women's work."

"As soon as I con someone into marrying me, I'll be in the living room watching TV while my wife slaves away out here."

"Thought so," she said sagely.

"Get back to those beans, woman." He yelped, and dodged the sharp point of her knife. Megan turned back to work with a satisfied grin.

When the meal—steaks with green salsa, beans and fried potatoes—was ready, they sat in the small dining room to eat. Travis lit a tall, thin candle in a brass candlestick. He uncorked a bottle of cabernet sauvignon and poured two glasses of the ruby wine.

They clinked glasses. "Here's to Martha Stewart," Travis said.

Megan sliced into her perfectly medium rare steak. She popped it into her mouth and closed her eyes to savor the taste. "This is great. I should cook more often."

"Find yourself a chauvinist husband, let him pressure you into giving up work, then you can cook as often as you want."

She smiled.

"Will you stay at Merritt, Merritt & Finch if your father doesn't give you his job?" Travis asked.

"Of course," she said. "I couldn't leave, I love that place." She sipped her wine. "Let's not talk work, Travis. That way, we can't have any conflict of interest."

He moved the candle aside, so there was nothing between them. "What do you want to talk about?"

Travis didn't want to talk at all. He barely wanted to eat. Having Megan here in his house, at his table, was an assault on his senses. Who would have thought that cooking and eating a simple steak dinner could feel so…significant.

Maybe he was subconsciously trying to salvage something from that disastrous meeting with Jonah. To make it worth screwing up.

"I figured out why you jumped in to help me with Dad this afternoon," she said.

He speared a piece of steak with his fork. "No, you didn't."

"You're having problems with your own father. The other day it seemed he was expecting something of you that you weren't delivering."

"You'd be a pain to live with," he observed. At the thought of *living with* Megan, he felt light-headed. He was drinking too fast.

She grinned. "Are my powers of perception dazzling you?"

"Scaring me," he corrected. "Remind me never to go up against you in a divorce."

She laughed. "You know about my problems with my dad, so tell me about yours."

"On the other hand, if that's your idea of logic, maybe I do stand a chance of beating you." He took a cautious drink of wine.

"Unlikely," she said. "Go on, tell me. I hate that you pity me."

Beneath the light tone, he sensed that she meant it. "Pity isn't what I feel for you," he said, then stopped. Because suddenly, he had no idea what he felt. In the candlelight, with fire crackling in the living room, attraction was the number one sentiment, if you could call it that. The vestiges of a smile curved her lips.

Probably just as well she didn't want to settle down and have kids, it would be a waste of one hell of a brain. He pulled himself up. *Say, what?*

She touched his wrist. "Tell me, Travis."

Had she ever touched him before? Touched him first? He could only assume not, because the flame that swept him like a brush fire took him totally by surprise.

Tightened his groin, loosened his lips.

"Mom and Dad have fallen out with some of their friends," he said. "Over me."

She stroked his wrist, coaxing him. "You broke their daughter's heart?"

He struggled to breathe. "Girl couldn't make apple pie worth a damn. She had to go."

Megan murmured sympathetically. "It's not easy being an old-fashioned guy."

She had no idea how right she was. How his caveman instincts made him want to sweep the meal off the table and haul her across the surface. "Mom and Dad have lived in Jackson Creek all their lives. It's one of those small towns with a huge community spirit. I couldn't have gone to college if the whole place hadn't been right behind me."

Megan sat back; instantly he missed her touch. She

lifted her wineglass to her lips but didn't drink. "How do you mean?"

He cut a bean and added it to his fork with a piece of potato. "As you figured the other day, Mom and Dad never had much cash. There was no way they could afford for me to get a law degree, even with a student loan. When I was accepted for college, the town chipped in. They fund-raised, they donated, they sold everything that wasn't nailed down on eBay to raise the cash."

"Incredible."

"It was an amazing gift," he agreed. "I told folks I'd pay them back one day, but of course they didn't want that. So a few years ago I set up a scholarship to do what they did for me—pay for a local kid to attend college each year."

"That's very decent," she said.

The scholarship was barely a blip in his bank balance. Money wasn't his problem.

"Did the town pay your brothers' college fees, too?" she asked.

"Clay went into construction straight from high school, and built up a successful business. He's doing college studies part-time now. Brent won a scholarship to Georgia State—these days he has his own consulting firm. The three of us are paying Gina's fees at Duke." Travis watched the flicker of shadows on her face in the candlelight. She would have always been destined to work in her dad's firm; she'd never had to think about carving a place for herself.

She pushed a piece of potato around her plate, mopping up some of the steak juices. If she knew how proprietary he felt, watching her eat food he'd prepared for her, food they'd created together, she would freak out. He was struggling not to freak out himself; his fork was slippery in his palm.

"So, what's the problem?" she asked.

"Everyone in Jackson Creek had faith in me to make it through college, to become an ace lawyer. My parents had double the faith of everyone put together."

"Lucky. I wish my dad had that much faith in me."

He flipped his knife between his fingers. "It's a two-edged sword. If you don't live up to people's expectations, they take it personally."

She was smart, she cottoned on right away. "People don't approve of you working for PPA?"

"It was only ever a temporary job," he said.

She raised her eyebrows. "You've been there ten years."

"Yeah, yeah."

"Your division at PPA is aboveboard." A statement, not a question.

Her belief in him warmed him through. "That's the justification I've always used, but it's not enough anymore. There's a couple in Jackson Creek, Doug and Mary Laing, they own a supermarket. Three months back, a tourist from Atlanta slipped in their store and broke his hip. He's suing them for a couple of mil."

"PPA is representing the plaintiff," Megan guessed.

"Yep. I didn't know anything about it—speculative personal injury lawsuits are as common as coffee around PPA—until Dad told me. The Laings are good friends of my parents. Or they were."

"Ouch."

"Doug and Mary did as much as anyone to get me into college. They don't have a bad bone in their bodies.

But the PPA associate on the case went digging for dirt. He found out that forty years ago Doug deserted from the army in Vietnam. Now it's all over town and the Laings are humiliated."

"So the people who scrimped and saved to send you to college feel as if their generosity is being thrown back in their faces," Megan summarized, with all the finesse she'd employ in a courtroom.

He put it more bluntly. "Folks think I've lost my integrity."

Her forehead creased. "Them saying it doesn't make it true." But she wasn't disagreeing, either.

He appreciated that she didn't rush to reassure him. "My parents raised me to put family first, to use my talents to serve my clients as best I can and to live with integrity," he said. "I bought into that not because I was brainwashed, but because I could see it worked. Mom and Dad are still blissfully happy together after nearly forty years, they have more integrity than anyone I know. The only thing that ever caused friction between them was occasional money worries. I wanted what they had, minus the financial difficulties. A job at a good firm…"

"And a happy family at home," she completed.

"That was the dream. Instead, my financial security is starting to feel like blood money, and I'm no nearer the home-and-hearth thing than I was when I started." The candle flame wavered as he exhaled, then steadied. "I've always known it, but until the Laings, it hasn't been urgent enough to do anything about. Now, people I care about are suffering. And my parents can't hold their heads up around town. I have to make some changes."

Megan wiped her mouth with her napkin, and immediately he focused on her lips. "I've seen you with your father, I've seen you with kids. It seems to me, you have plenty of integrity."

"Thanks." He just about gagged on the word. She wouldn't say that if she knew why they were involved in the Hoskins case together.

"Why did you join PPA in the first place?" she asked.

Travis hadn't discussed that old business in years. He took a sip of wine and let the mellow warmth spread through him. "You could say I was repaying a debt. Kyle Prescott saved my life."

CHAPTER TEN

THE FACT THAT TRAVIS WAS sitting across the dinner table from her, demonstrably alive and well, did nothing to stop Megan's visceral reaction to the news that at one point his life had needed saving.

Somehow, she managed to set down her knife and fork, as if they were talking about nothing more important than the court schedule. "How exactly—" *breathe* "—did Kyle save your life?"

"We were students, out on a bender, and I was the designated driver," he said. "It was my turn, that's all. We were driving back to the dorm, a truck crossed the centerline and pushed the car off the road into a culvert. A damned deep one. The truck driver had fallen asleep. He was later found guilty of manslaughter."

His wooden tone didn't begin to conceal the horror he must have gone through that night. Megan's stomach roiled.

"Kyle didn't have his seat belt on—he was in the back and he was thrown clear," Travis continued. "That guy has the luck of the devil. He landed on a pile of clippings, instead of hitting his head on the concrete." He swirled the wine in his glass, stared into it. "Steve, the guy in the passenger seat—I hadn't met him before that night—died instantly. Another guy in the back managed to crawl out. I was trapped, unconscious and bleeding heavily."

"And Kyle helped you?"

"I'd swear he was drunk as a skunk, but somehow he dragged me out of there, made a tourniquet to stop the bleeding and called nine-one-one. I stopped breathing at one point, the paramedics told me later, and Kyle gave me mouth-to-mouth."

Megan's salsa threatened to make a reappearance. "That's…impressive," she managed to say.

He patted her hand. "Kyle is an odd guy. Reckless and driven and selfish, yet he has this rescuer complex at the unlikeliest moments. Before the accident, I barely knew him. Afterward, I was proud to count him as a friend."

"I imagine he's the kind of guy who wouldn't hesitate to take advantage of that."

He opened his mouth as if to defend Prescott. Then he shrugged. "I guess. Kyle got fired from his first job for falsifying his time sheets, so he set up his own firm with Jim Palmer. They took the cases no one else wanted and they were both accomplished lawyers— they grew like crazy. When Kyle's parents died, he fell apart. He asked me to come in and help. I was working in Dallas back then, but I didn't hesitate."

She studied his face. "And you're still there."

"Kyle wasn't the only one to benefit from the deal. I have free rein in the property division and it's a strong business. I might even make more money than you do."

"I admire your loyalty," she said. "But what happens now?" She toyed with a piece of wax that had fallen from the candle. "Will you look for a new job?"

He sat back. "I'd like to join a blue-chip firm."

"Oh," she said doubtfully.

"Exactly," he agreed. "Ex-PPA partners aren't high on the list of desirable employees. Atlanta has some of the stuffiest law firms in the country. If you can't trace your lineage back to the Confederacy…"

"Some of them are more evenhanded," she said. "Look at my dad. Even being his daughter isn't enough to win me any favors." She rolled the piece of wax between her fingers. His story explained his edginess, the tension she'd sensed at the sandwich bar. Nothing to do with her, or Theo—she was ashamed of her suspicions. "There must be some way for you to get into a more reputable firm."

"Don't worry about me," he said roughly. "I have it in hand."

She poured water from the jug on the table into her glass, then his. "I hope you get what you want, Travis. You deserve it."

"I thought we agreed not to talk about work."

She sipped her water. "Okay, let's talk about Christmas. Will you spend it with your family?"

"Of course. It's a protracted event at our place. The festivities always kick off with the town's Christmas social on the last Saturday in November—that's this weekend. Then there's the traditional wild boar hunt. There aren't any wild boars around, but it gives people an excuse to go thundering through the woods before they buy a pig from the butcher and roast it on a spit. Then we have cake-and-eggnog night at church. By the time the twenty-fifth rolls around, we're too tired to move."

She laughed. "It sounds quaint."

"That's probably the right word. I guess a Merritt family Christmas is a little more sophisticated."

"We start with the firm's party, which is next week."

"That's business," he objected.

"It's a big night for all of us, including Sabrina, who's never worked at Merritt, Merritt & Finch. We're pretty busy with corporate entertaining, right up until the office closes for the holiday. We go to some family friends, the Warringtons, for Christmas dinner."

"Lucky, judging by your culinary abilities."

"My sister Sabrina is a Cordon Bleu cook." She drained her wineglass. "Which reminds me, I need to pick up the brûlée torch I ordered her for Christmas. I haven't even started my shopping."

"You have a lot on your mind." Travis gathered up the plates. "How's your promotion-by-coffee strategy going?"

"Stealthily," she admitted.

"Do you really think your dad cares what you drink?"

"You'll know from any jury trial how the least significant things can substantially alter someone's perception," she said. "In Dad's view, serious players drink espresso. I'm creating the right impression." She followed him to the kitchen, where he switched on the coffee machine.

"So you're still afraid of lattes?"

She pulled a face.

"Espresso, then?" He scooped grounds into the filter basket.

"I don't exactly like it, but I crave it," she confessed. "I don't know what I like anymore." She took two mugs from the hooks on the wall. "Do you have any tea? Hot tea?"

When Travis had made the drinks, they took them to the living room, and sat on the couch. Megan clasped her mug in both hands and sipped at it. "This isn't too bad. I wonder what Dad thinks about tea drinkers."

"Beats me why he can't just see what an asset he has in you," Travis said.

Her insides melted like snow in a spring thaw. "Thanks."

He set his cup down on the coffee table, next to the Christmas wreath in the center. He untwisted a sprig of plastic mistletoe.

"Travis," Megan warned, as he held it over her head.

"It's a tradition, and I'm a traditional kind of guy." He took her cup, put it on the table.

"Prehistoric, you mean." But she didn't move away. "That thing isn't even real."

"*This* is real," he said, and lowered his lips to hers.

His groan as his mouth closed over hers echoed deep inside Megan. His touch trailed down her spine, as he pressed the small of her back so that she leaned more intimately into him, as he cupped her rear before brushing her skirt against the back of her thighs.

She had never, ever felt this scalding heat in a man's arms. A heat that provoked her into action. Greedily, she tugged his shirt out of his pants, explored the firm flesh of his torso.

Travis groaned. "Megs..." He lifted her hair, nuzzling her neck. "You're so beautiful."

She tipped her head back, inviting his caress. He made her *feel* beautiful. More beautiful than Sabrina. Stronger than Cynthia. She discarded the comparisons, didn't need them. Travis saw *her*, he wanted *her*.

He undid the top two buttons of her pin-striped blouse and pushed aside the collar. "I recall you saying you want to go to bed."

She sighed with pleasure at the tickle of his tongue. "I meant alone."

"So delectably prim," he murmured.

"Travis, we need to be professional…oh!" He'd nipped her collarbone; she arched against him.

"Consider me professionally turned-on," he said. "Did it occur to you that going to bed *not* alone could be so much more fun."

She wriggled against him, and he groaned. "I don't do…*that* for fun," she said.

"Me neither. At least, not *just* for fun. With you, this would be…" He trailed off, all his concentration going into kissing her shoulder.

Dangerous, she thought. *Beyond all my experience.* She wanted it.

She tugged at him until he brought his mouth back up to hers, and she kissed him deeply.

"Megan," he said. She loved that she'd put that desperate hoarseness in his voice. "Make love with me."

Very softly, she said, "Okay."

TRAVIS DREW BACK and stared at her to make sure he'd heard right. No mistaking the mischief in her smile, the promise in her eyes.

Yes!

He kissed her again. He stood, pulling her to her feet. "Upstairs."

He linked his fingers with hers, trying not to drag her in his impatience. She seemed to be in the same hurry—she bumped into him at the foot of the stairs. A breathy laugh escaped her.

A voice in Travis's head was trying to tell him something he didn't want to hear. He shut it out and took the stairs two at a time, pulling Megan along.

But the damned voice persisted. *You can't make love to her without telling her the truth.*

Hell. He stopped dead on the landing, and she bumped into him again. How had he come to this? Had he been working at PPA so long that he'd lost his morality?

"I think it's that way." Megan pointed down the hall.

He *was* lost, dammit. Travis cursed himself for not having told her earlier that he wanted to head her dad's firm. Now, his admission would be a huge betrayal of trust, no matter that neither of them was actually in the running for the job. No matter that they hadn't actually made love yet.

"Travis?" She tugged his sleeve.

He looked down at her, and wondered how he could ever have thought she wasn't particularly pretty. The sparkle in her eyes, the curve of her cheek, the tilt of her chin, her beautiful neck…everything about her was perfect. Her sense of humor, her dedication to her work, her modesty, her honesty…

"What's wrong?" She was so close to him, her breath fanned his lips, turning his ache for her into something nearer agony.

He pulled her against him, burying his nose in her sweet-smelling hair. "Megs, we can't do this."

She swayed in his embrace, tempting him all over again, then eased away. "The Hoskinses…I can't believe I almost forgot about the case. Our professional conflict of interest."

The Hoskinses? He'd *completely* forgotten them.

She pulled out of his arms with a shaky laugh. "I guess I should thank you for the reminder."

"Don't thank me," he said roughly.

She buried her face in her hands. "Travis, this was such a bad idea."

"You're right." And she didn't know the half of it.

"We need—" she took a careful step back and grasped the newel post at the top of the stairs "—to cool it."

He needed a cold shower, that was for sure. "You're right," he repeated.

Her smile was perplexed. "It's not like you to agree with me."

He ran a hand around the back of his neck. "This is the first time we've covered this subject."

"First and last time," she suggested.

"You can't just shut off the attraction, Megs."

But maybe he was wrong, because her expression was cooling right in front of him. "I can ignore it. So can you."

"Fine," he said, "we'll ignore it." *For now.*

TRAVIS SNEAKED up behind his mom as she stood at the kitchen counter stirring some kind of mixture in one of her old china mixing bowls. He knew exactly which floorboards creaked in the bungalow in Jackson Creek where his parents had lived the last forty-odd years, so he achieved maximum stealth.

That didn't stop Ellie Jamieson from saying, as he got almost within arm's reach, "Hello, Travis, honey."

He hugged his mother from behind. "I thought those eyes in the back of your head might have been closed." He'd been trying to sneak up on her since he was six years old, and had never once succeeded.

"Not a chance." She turned to embrace him. "It's wonderful to see you."

It was a warmer welcome than he deserved. "You, too. What's cooking?"

"Can you believe I only just got around to making my Christmas cake?"

"Scandalous," he said, and wished he hadn't. That word had been bandied around enough in this town lately. In connection with him. "Is Dad around?"

"He's helping decorate the hall." Ellie poured her mixture into a paper-lined cake pan, scraping every last bit from the bowl. She tapped the wooden spoon sharply on the edge of the pan. "He shouldn't be, with that new hip, but you know what he's like."

There was no civic cause too trivial for Hugh to lend his assistance. Unlike Jonah Merritt, a big shot in Atlanta, Hugh had never earned much money. But he'd left his mark on the town in countless ways.

"Clay's around somewhere." Clay still lived in Jackson Creek. "And Brent will be here later, but Gina called to say she's not coming this weekend at all." Ellie hid her disappointment by turning and sliding the cake into the oven. "I guess she's seeing that boyfriend of hers."

"Don't you like him?" Travis had planned to talk to Gina this weekend, as his father had suggested. Obviously that wasn't about to happen.

"He's nice enough, but I worry that he's rushing her." Travis lent her a hand stacking her baking utensils in the dishwasher. "I wish she'd bring him here, so we can see what they're up to."

Travis suspected that was exactly why Gina didn't bring Scott to Jackson Creek. He wedged the last of the dirty cutlery into the basket. "I'll go find Dad."

"Lunch in half an hour," Ellie said. "I made oxtail soup." His favorite.

"Thanks, Ma." He kissed her cheek and left.

If the Jackson Creek community hall didn't look much like the Santa's workshop it was meant to be for the Christmas social each year, it wasn't due to a lack of enthusiasm. A bevy of workers strung tinsel, blew up balloons and festooned lights around the walls. It was, as Megan had said, quaint.

He missed her. It had been three days since he'd decided to ignore the heat between them, and he hadn't been able to forget it for one second.

Brian Hill and Stewart Dobson, two of Travis's dad's oldest friends, were setting up the bar near the kitchen. Travis stopped to greet them, though he would have preferred to walk on by. But these guys had once been his biggest supporters. Sometimes, Travis wished his career wasn't seen as public property in Jackson Creek. But then you had to take the bad with the good. He couldn't ignore the old guys, much as they'd probably like him to.

Their return greetings bordered on curt. After a short silence, Stewart said, "You still with that PPA crowd?" As if a change of job wouldn't have been broadcast all over town within minutes.

"Yep. Still heading up the property division." As opposed to the sleaze division. The distinction would cut no ice around here.

Stewart sucked in his cheeks, cueing another silence.

"I've come to pick up Dad," Travis said.

Brian pointed across the hall. "Over there."

Travis found his father up a ladder, hanging the last of eight plastic reindeer from a beam.

"Don't tell your mother," Hugh said when he saw Travis.

"My lips are sealed." Travis steadied the ladder while his dad secured Dasher's wire—or was it Dancer's?—then climbed down.

Hugh dusted his hands off on his pants before he clapped Travis on the shoulder. "You're early. That brother of yours won't be here until five."

"I wanted to talk to you and Mom," Travis said, "and I know it'll turn crazy later." Doubtless his mom would be chief caterer tonight, and Dad would be barkeep.

Back at home, Ellie ladled soup into the seventies geometric-patterned bowls he'd grown up with, while his dad opened a couple of cans of Bud—obviously this week's special at the liquor store. His parents were careful. Frugal. They didn't break bowls, and they shopped on a tight budget. Offers of a little cash from their children were firmly rebuffed.

"Dad, Mom, I have some news you won't like." Travis had come to the decision on his way here that he couldn't keep his parents' hopes up.

Hugh slurped his soup, grimacing apologetically to his wife. "Go ahead."

"I know how keen you are for me to leave PPA...but it's not going to happen anytime soon."

"I see." Hugh put down his spoon and sat back.

"It was always a long shot," Travis said. He should have known better than to mention the Merritt, Merritt & Finch opportunity. Thankfully he hadn't told them about all the other attempts he'd made the past few months to get into one of the top firms, *any* of the top firms. Working the phones, calling contacts, searching out opportunities. Only to be knocked down every time.

Travis took a long swallow of his beer. "When I

joined PPA, I told you it would be three years, max, and then I'd go work for a decent firm. I've let you and Mom down. Not to mention everyone else around here."

"You had your reasons," his father said. "Your mom and I understand why you went to work for that fellow." The implication being that others in the close-knit town didn't. Hugh rubbed his wedding band. "It's true we'd rather see you in a firm that fits with the kind of man we know you are, but any problems in town here are as much our fault as yours."

"If we'd had more money," Ellie chipped in, "we'd have sent you to college ourselves, and it would be no one else's business where you work."

"Not that it is anyway." Hugh scrubbed at a glass mark on his place mat with his cotton napkin. "Your mother's right, we haven't been able to give any of you kids much, to our regret."

"Dad…" Travis dropped his own soupspoon, and it clattered into the bowl, spraying oxtail soup onto the table. "None of that money stuff mattered. You guys gave us the happiest childhood imaginable. You taught us what's really important. I managed to screw up all by myself."

"So, you still want the same things out of life?" Ellie asked. "A wife and kids who'll be your top priority?"

"If I can do half as good a parenting job as you, I'll be a happy man," he promised.

Ellie stood and ladled more soup into his bowl from the pot she'd brought to the middle of the table. "Your father told me you were with a girl when he saw you in the city. A lawyer."

No mistaking the worry in her voice, worry that he would screw up on the personal front, too.

"Nothing's going on, Mom," he assured her. And that was official.

"I have to admit I'm relieved," Ellie said. "Your father said that girl came right out and said she doesn't want kids."

"It's complicatcd." The urge to defend Megan was still strong.

"It's not that complicated, dear. I'm not saying she may not have her reasons, just like you, but that doesn't change things."

"Yeah, you're right." Suddenly, Travis was sick of everyone being right about him and Megan being a bad idea.

CHAPTER ELEVEN

BY NINE O'CLOCK the Jackson Creek hall was busting at the seams.

The town's leading—and only—rock band, the Jackson Jive, had kicked off with a series of eighties hits that got everyone onto the dance floor. Travis had danced with an assortment of women, mostly old classmates. By the time the band segued into *"Unchained Melody,"* a dreary song women seemed to love, he was ready for a break.

He headed for the bar, only to bump into his parents coming the other way.

"We're just going to have a dance," his mom said.

"Your mother's favorite tune." Hugh scowled, but didn't resist.

At the bar, a makeshift arrangement of trestle tables, Travis found his brothers, Brent and Clay. They ordered a round of whiskies, including one for him, with a beer chaser.

Travis led the way to one of the hired pub tables, where he set down his drinks. "How're the boys?" he asked Clay. The middle Jamieson son was the only one to have taken the plunge into matrimony. Their parents had been devastated for him when his marriage broke up.

As always, Clay's stern expression lifted at the mention of his kids. "They're with Laura."

His brother had to practically beg his ex-wife to take the kids for one measly weekend a year. No wonder he looked so cranky. Travis eyed him critically. Clay was good-looking, and back in high school he'd had more girls after him than he could handle. But he hadn't dated in a long time. Maybe he needed a woman to drive out his bad memories.

"You seeing anyone?" Travis asked.

Clay shook his head. "Don't get much time, between work and the boys."

Travis checked out the local talent over the rim of his glass. "What about Tracey Wells?" Clay's high school sweetheart was swaying to "Unchained Melody" while she talked with a friend.

"No chemistry."

"Sue McIntosh?"

"She just got married."

Travis's gaze swept the room, searching.

"Leave it, Travis," Clay said. "I'm happy as I am."

Brent traded a dubious look with Travis.

"I assume you're still keeping up your playboy habits," Travis asked his youngest brother.

"What makes you think that?" Brent raised his beer bottle and winked at a blonde who'd just lurched into one of the bar trestle tables, making it wobble.

"That's Mrs. Carson's granddaughter," Travis warned him. "I hear chronic flatulence is hereditary in women."

That made Clay chuckle, which was something. "How about you, Travis?" Clay asked. "Dad said you're 'seeing' someone." He grinned. "I figured he meant boinking."

"I'm not boinking her," Travis said sharply, conscious of how nearly he had been.

Both his brothers shifted into a state of alertness. "Sounds serious," Brent said.

"Only you would think *not* sleeping with a woman was a sign of a meaningful relationship," Travis said, unable to shake images of Megan in his arms, in his bed.

"I'm not you. You're the guy who always wanted to do it right." Brent gulped down his whisky. "Find yourself an old-fashioned girl, have her tend the kids and the picket fence while you do your lawyer thing."

"Are you serious about this woman?" Clay asked.

"I'm not even dating her. She's a colleague."

"A lawyer?" Clay said, horrified.

"Yes, a lawyer. She's a friend."

Brent hooted. "First she's a colleague, then she's a friend. What's next—lovers?"

Clay wasn't so amused. "So let's get this straight. You haven't done anything with this woman that you wouldn't do with any other lawyer. Say, with Kyle Prescott."

On the dance floor, "Unchained Melody" came to a merciful end, the band moving into "Kissing You." "It's none of your damn business." Travis had a sudden inkling why Megan objected so emphatically to his questioning her about her dates.

Clay's jaw set. "I don't want you to make the same mistake I did."

Travis tossed back his whisky. Through the burn he said, "It's nothing like that. Megan's made it clear she doesn't want kids."

His attempt to make her look honest and transparent backfired. Clay's chin dropped, and even Brent looked worried.

"This woman told you she doesn't want the same thing you do, and you're still seeing her?" Brent said. "That would be like me dating a woman who was desperate to get married and settle down. Are you deceiving her, or just plain stupid?"

"I'm not even dating her," Travis ground out.

"Don't do it," Clay said. "If you think you can change her mind down the track, I'm living proof it doesn't work."

"Megan isn't Laura."

Uh-oh.

Clay set his beer down on the pub table, unconsciously flexing his right bicep. At least, Travis hoped it was unconscious. His brother still did enough physical labor to be in peak condition, where Travis hadn't found time to get to the gym in months.

"What's that supposed to mean?" Clay demanded.

Travis wasn't about to admit he'd never liked his sister-in-law.

Brent intervened. "So what *is* Megan like, then?"

Travis started on his beer. "She's...a little uptight. Ambitious. Keeps to herself. Quiet, mostly."

Brent scratched his head. "And this is a woman you *like?*"

"It *is* serious," Clay said. "I can't believe you're about to wreck your love life, after the mess you made of your career, joining that scumbag firm."

Brent sucked in a breath and clamped his hand tighter around his beer. "Guys, let's just have a friendly drink."

"And now you're getting involved with a woman who doesn't want kids. When are you going to do the right thing, like you always tell us to?"

Unable to think of an answer, Travis glanced at Brent for support.

His brother grimaced. "And to think I used to feel guilty when you gave me that do-the-right-thing lecture. For Pete's sake, Travis, learn from Clay's idiocy. Dump this Megan chick now."

Travis fought the urge to punch his brother in his dimpled chin. Over a woman he wasn't even dating and he knew damn well was wrong for him!

"Would this family please butt out?" he muttered. "No wonder Gina doesn't want to come home."

His cell phone rang, and he pounced on the opportunity to escape. He checked the display: Barbara Hoskins's home number. "A client," he told Clay, who rolled his eyes.

Travis picked up as he headed outside. The cold night air socked him the punch he needed to shake off his aggravation. "Barbara, what's up?"

"Um, it's Marcus here," said a childish voice.

Travis walked down the wide concrete steps, farther away from the music. The clock tower above the hall read ten o'clock. "Marcus, you're up late, buddy."

"I can't find Mom."

Alarm whistled through Travis like a December wind. "What do you mean?" he asked slowly.

"Chelsea woke up with a stomachache. She went to tell Mom, but she's not here. I've looked all over. Her purse is gone, but her cell phone's on the charger." The boy's voice had gotten higher with every sentence until he ended in a squeak.

"Okay, buddy, we'll find her," Travis said. "Did you try your dad?"

"He's not home, and he's not answering his cell

phone. I left him some messages. Your number is on the wall next to the phone, so I called you."

"Okay, good boy." Travis paced to the sundial in the middle of the quadrangle. Barbara wasn't the kind of woman to leave her kids home alone. What the hell was going on?

And what should he tell Marcus? He knew the Hoskinses didn't have any family in Atlanta, and he was reluctant to have Marcus start phoning his parents' friends. If Travis left now, he'd be back in Atlanta around midnight...but the kids couldn't wait that long. Call the police? The media would be all over the scandal like gravy over biscuits.

"Marcus, I'm out of town," he said. The boy heaved a sob, which all but broke Travis's heart. "I'll call Megan," he hurried on. It was far from ideal, but at least the kids knew her. There was no chance of keeping this from her anyway, given Marcus had left his dad those undoubtedly terrified messages. "She'll come and stay with you until we find your parents, okay?"

If he could get hold of her. In the background, he could hear Chelsea questioning Marcus incessantly. The boy was holding up for her sake, Travis guessed.

He arranged to call back using a coded ring since Marcus was anxious about answering the phone to a stranger at night, reassured the boy one more time, then said goodbye.

He hit speed dial for Megan.

"Hello?" She sounded alert, wide awake.

"Are you on a date?" he blurted.

"I don't believe this," she said grimly.

Hell. "Sorry," he said. "I didn't mean that the way

it sounded. I had a call from Marcus." Quickly, he outlined the situation.

"Travis, that's awful. Those poor kids." He could hear from her voice that she was already on the move. "I'll go over there right away."

"Thanks. Look for any clues as to where Barbara might be. An invitation on the fridge, or a diary note. She left her cell at home, so there's not a lot else we can do to find her."

"I'd better try Theo, too." She was right, of course. The kids needed a parent, any parent, more than they needed Megan or Travis. "I'll call you as soon as I have news," she promised.

"Thanks," he said again. "Doesn't matter how late."

After he called Marcus to confirm Megan was on her way, Travis hung around outside, wishing there was more he could do. Twenty minutes later, Megan called to say she was at Barbara's house, and the kids were fine.

"Chelsea's stomachache seems better, so I'll put them back to bed. Do you think they're too old for a story?"

"Borderline, but I'm sure it'll go down well when they're upset." Then, because he wanted to prolong the conversation, he added, "But you realize kids their age need an original story, minimum twenty minutes, featuring them in starring roles, and acted out with costumes by the storyteller. Right?"

Dead silence. "They're getting a chapter of *Harry Potter*. So sue me."

He snickered. "You're the boss."

"Damn right," she said. "I'm going to move Marcus into the spare bed in Chelsea's room. They'll both appreciate the company."

"Whatever you say." He saluted, even though she couldn't see him.

"So…how's the Jackson Creek social?" she asked.

"The usual," he said. "Drinking, dancing. We'll probably get to auld lang syne at some stage."

A pause. "Who did you dance with?"

His senses pricked up. Was it possible he wasn't the only one capable of jealousy? "A couple of girls I went to high school with."

"Hmm. I guess they'd be quite old now."

"Older than you," he agreed. "But they still have all their hair."

She snorted a half laugh. "You're an idiot."

"I know," he said with a humility that made her laugh for real. Man, he loved that sound.

"Stop being cute," she ordered.

"I can't," he said in the same tone.

She hung up, leaving him grinning into the phone like a loon.

Which was stupid. He pocketed the phone as he turned back to the hall. Clay was right. Even Brent was right, dammit, and his younger brother was the last person to listen to on personal matters. Travis had no business flirting with Megan.

He needed to go back to Atlanta and fight for Jonah's job with everything he had.

CHAPTER TWELVE

TRAVIS'S CELL RANG at three in the morning. He rolled over in his half-awake state and grabbed his phone. "Megan?" He heard arguing in the background. "Barbara's back?"

"And Theo." She sounded exhausted, slurring her words. He'd bet she hadn't slept at all. "They got here at the same time."

"Where were they?" Travis sat up in the single bed he'd grown up sleeping in, and pushed the blankets aside.

"Theo was at a rock concert, he didn't hear his phone over the music."

Way to go, Theo, great time to start reliving your youth. Travis walked to the window. The carpeted floor was much warmer underfoot than his floorboards in the city. He hadn't closed the curtains, and the pale moon lit the room. "And Barbara?"

Behind Megan, the arguing intensified. "Just a moment, Travis." She must have covered the phone with her hand, because her voice was muffled, but not so muffled that he couldn't hear. "Shut up, you two, you'll wake the kids."

The sudden background silence was probably more shock than obedience, he suspected. Travis grinned at the moon.

"I'll take this to the kitchen," she said, and there was a pause while she moved out of the Hoskinses' earshot.

"Barbara did knowingly go out and leave the kids home alone," Megan said.

Travis's heart sank.

"She'd planned a late dinner with her boyfriend," Megan continued, "because she didn't want to go out before the kids were in bed. She had a sitter arranged for nine, but right before Barbara was supposed to leave, the sitter called to say she'd be ten minutes late."

"I can guess what comes next."

"The kids were asleep, so Barbara figured they'd be fine on their own until the sitter arrived." Her voice sounded low and intimate, as if she'd brought the phone closer to her mouth. Her lips were so clear in his mind, it was as if she was right there with him.

"But for some reason the sitter didn't turn up." Travis rested his forehead on the windowpane. Below, his mom's garden was in shadow.

"Her car broke down. She left a message on Barbara's cell, not realizing Barbara had left the phone at home." Megan paused. "Barbara's very upset."

"She should be," Travis said. A tiny sound came down the phone; he recognized it as the peak of a yawn.

"Travis, Theo has asked me to seek an interim custody order first thing Monday."

MEGAN SELDOM SUFFERED from nerves in the courtroom. She made a point of being more prepared than her competition knew it was possible to be, and that was enough to give her confidence.

Not today. The first test of how well her efforts were serving Theo was also the first time she'd been on the opposite side of a courtroom from Travis. While she was convinced her case was strong, she had no idea what to expect from him. Unlike most of the lawyers she faced off against, he was unpredictable.

Her father sat in the back of the courtroom, unwittingly ramping Megan's stress levels sky-high.

Despite Barbara's lapse in judgment on Saturday night, Megan was coming from behind, arguing Theo should have custody of the children. Although the courts claimed equal treatment, they still tended to favor mothers.

She checked through her files for the twelfth time. She had everything she needed. Travis sat at the table across the aisle, immaculate in his dark suit, white shirt, bronze tie. He was sprawled back in his chair, the way he'd been the first day she saw him. He looked as if he was prepared for no more than lifting a finger to order a beer.

On Megan's right, Theo flipped his BlackBerry over and over in his fingers. "Can we win this?" he asked, as clients always did when last-minute anxiety attacked.

She'd never answered that question with a no, and she wasn't about to now. "We can," she said. "We will."

The mantra steadied her as she rose along with everyone else for Judge Sylvia Teague to enter. Judge Teague was, like Barbara, a mother of two and a career woman. She was also divorced. Megan couldn't be sure if the judge would come down hard on a woman who had let down her side, or if she would be sympathetic toward Barbara's attempts to juggle her life.

Briefly, Megan wondered what kind of judge her sister Cynthia would make. The conflict of interest meant she wouldn't be allowed to hear Megan's cases. Just as well—Cynthia was so devoted to her work she'd probably give Megan an extrahard time just to prove she wasn't favoring her.

Since Megan's client had requested the interim custody hearing, she was up first.

She put Theo on the stand and led him through his testimony, starting with, "Tell the court about the phone calls you received from your son on Saturday night." She presented her case simply and clearly. That Barbara Hoskins, by going out to meet her lover before the babysitter arrived, had shown herself unfit to care for the children. And that they would therefore be better off with their father.

Of course, that wasn't the end of the story.

Travis stood. "Your Honor," he began, and Megan's spine tingled. "I have some questions for Mr. Hoskins."

Travis's cross-examination elicited what they both knew: that Theo had been unreachable because he was at a rock concert, that he'd taken a cab to Barbara's house because he was drunk or, as Megan corrected him in her objection, he'd exceeded the legal alcohol limit for driving. Thank goodness custody hearings were closed to the media.

Next, Theo was obliged to admit that last week, when Barbara had been away on business, he'd been unable to have the kids because he, too, was out of town. Barbara had cut her trip short because she didn't want to leave the kids with a sitter for more than one night. A model mother, was Travis's implication.

Maybe it was the lack of sleep as a result of putting together a custody suit at such short notice, but right now, Megan was ineffably weary of the whole case.

Why couldn't the Hoskinses have put a bit more work into their marriage, for the sake of their kids?

She watched Travis as he questioned Theo. He looked every bit as fatigued as she did, but on him it lent a rugged effect. Typical.

As Travis spoke to the judge, she sensed that he'd done the same research she had into Judge Teague's background. The judge was nodding unconsciously as he described the difficulties of carving out some personal time when you were a single mom and how gut-wrenching it was to leave your children with an alcoholic father—

Megan sprang to her feet. "Objection, Your Honor. Mr. Hoskins has never been labeled an alcoholic by anyone other than the wife who wants custody of his children. He strenuously denies any form of alcohol addiction."

"Sustained," the judge said. "Mr. Jamieson, please confine your argument to the facts." But her tone said *You naughty, handsome boy.*

Travis's smiling, faux-embarrassed apology didn't fool Megan for one second. This man was dangerous.

She forced herself to focus on the argument he presented, and got in a couple more good objections. After the second one, he shot her a look that gave her a greater sense of triumph than many wins she could remember.

Judge Teague retired to consider the arguments—the urgent nature of the case required an immediate decision. Megan had no idea which way the verdict would go. Her father shrugged. Not clear enough for him to call.

She and Theo paced together in the foyer. There was no sign of Barbara and Travis.

The call to return came an hour later. Uncharacteristically, Megan wasn't sure if a speedy decision was a good sign or a bad one.

Judge Teague began summing up by complimenting both attorneys on the clarity of their arguments. In an agony of suspense, Megan could only manage a taut smile. The judge went on to list what she considered the most salient points.

"This is a difficult decision," she concluded. "But on balance, I find in favor of Mr. Theo Hoskins, and award him full custody of the children."

Megan had won! Relief gushed through her, leaving her washed-out and shaky.

Theo pumped her hand, beaming. "You were wonderful, Megan. This means so much…thank you." His voice trembled.

"I'm happy for you." Megan tried to ignore Barbara's sobs. Travis put an arm around his client.

Theo had the grace to look discomfited. "I think I should have you with me when I go pick up the kids tonight."

Megan shivered. "Of course."

"I need to get ready for them, buy some food." Theo flicked through his BlackBerry messages as he spoke. "I'll be ready by five."

"Fine." Megan packed her briefcase. "And, Theo?"

He glanced up from the BlackBerry. "Hmm?"

"Do us all a favor," she said, "and clear out your liquor cabinet before the kids arrive."

He reddened. Then he nodded.

TRAVIS WAS ALSO PRESENT for the hand-over of the kids, which went surprisingly smoothly. If you didn't look too closely at Marcus's white face and Chelsea's confusion.

By the time Theo pulled away from curb with the children buckled securely into his Volvo, and Barbara closed her front door with a bang, Megan was drained.

"You realize we'll have to go through all that again soon," Travis said. "Barbara plans to appeal."

"That figures. I don't even know if the judge made the right decision. Which is better for the kids, the alcoholic or the adulterer?" Megan headed toward her BMW, parked in front of Travis's truck.

"It's grim," he agreed. He stopped her with a hand on her arm. "You did a great job for your client in court today."

"Thanks. So did you."

"But you won."

"It was a close-run thing. Even my dad said so."

He paused, his finger on the button of his remote control. Then he pressed down. The truck's lights flashed, but Travis stayed where he was, with her. "When did your father say that?"

"I talked to him before I left the courthouse. He was impressed with your performance." Jonah had complimented Megan on the win, but he'd also warned her how close she'd come to losing. To Travis.

Travis gazed into the distance. "Does your victory put you in a better position to get that job?"

"Are you kidding? Right after he congratulated me, Dad came out and told me I'm still not in the running." She rubbed her tired eyes.

"You're okay with that?" His dark eyes were opaque.

"Of course not, but it wasn't unexpected. I still have my plan to get myself on his short list."

"And that plan is…?" Travis prompted.

Too far-fetched to share. She changed the subject. "I've been thinking about what you said. About your need to get away from PPA."

His expression closed over, wiped as clean as one of those peel-back magic slate toys. Did he regret sharing those confidences?

She looked down at her keys. "Would you like to come to the Merritt, Merritt & Finch Christmas party tomorrow?"

CHAPTER THIRTEEN

TRAVIS COULDN'T AFFORD to blow this chance to redeem himself with Megan's father. He'd started this race from behind, then been put back a lap, thanks to his big mouth the last time he'd met Jonah. Was Jonah the kind to hold a grudge?

He stayed up most of the night working through every permutation of conversation that might take place between him and Jonah. Primed with coffee, he rehearsed again all the next day, the day of the party, except for a short break to get a haircut.

He'd just perfected his bow tie in front of his bedroom mirror—Jonah always looked dapper, and Megan's theory about first impressions was compelling—when his phone rang.

"You called?" His sister's voice came down the line.

"About a hundred times," he said, irritated that Gina had chosen now to finally get back to him.

"I've been busy."

"With your studies, I hope." Travis held the phone between his shoulder and his ear while he slipped one arm into his jacket. He swapped sides and did the other arm.

"Whatever," Gina said.

That didn't sound like his normally amenable sister.

"So, how are you doing?" He checked his reflection. In his tuxedo, he looked as if he'd fit right in at Merritt, Merritt & Finch.

"Did the folks ask you to check up on me?"

Man, she sounded as suspicious as Megan.

"They're worried about you," Travis said.

That was all it took for Gina to explode.

"This is so frigging pathetic," she ranted. "All I did was grow up, and Mom and Dad can't handle it. I'm eighteen years old, and they don't trust me to make decisions about my life."

"What kind of decisions?" Travis asked.

She ignored him. "Just because they don't like Scott, they're so mean about him."

"Maybe they need to get to know him better."

"They do know him. They think he's too old for me."

"How old is he?" He wrestled with a cuff link.

"Twenty-four," she mumbled.

Travis dropped the cuff link. It rolled beneath his dresser. He cursed as he crouched to get it.

"It's not that much older than I am." Gina misinterpreted the curse.

"Old enough." Travis groped under the dresser. His hand was almost too big for the gap. Dammit, how far could a cuff link roll?

"We love each other," she said.

His fingers closed around the cuff link. Carefully, he dragged it out. "That's nice." Then he registered her tone. "Why do you say that with such finality?"

"You're so suspicious, you're just like Dad."

"How can I take your side with Mom and Dad, if you won't tell me what's going on?" He started again with the cuff link. Pushing the round head through the buttonhole wasn't hard, it was the post that was fiddly.

"Scott asked me to marry him," Gina said.

"What?" He dropped the cuff link again.

"I'm thinking about saying yes," Gina said, a fraction less certainty in her voice.

"Don't you dare," Travis ordered. "You're too young." Dad would hit the roof if she dropped out of school. He glanced at the clock on his nightstand. Six-fifteen. Dammit, the party started at six-thirty and he wanted to be there before the masses, so he could reach Jonah before he was surrounded.

"Scott has a good job. We can afford to get married."

"Are you pregnant?"

"No, I'm not, you jerk." She added a couple of curse words.

"Watch your language." He was too conscious of the time to tell her off properly. "If you're not pregnant, then there's no rush. I have to go out now—I'll call you tomorrow."

By the time he hung up, he was so frazzled he'd be lucky to string a sentence together when he met Jonah.

THE MERRITT, MERRITT & Finch Christmas extravaganza took place in the Grand Lobby of Atlanta's High Museum of Art.

The enormous space's coffered ceiling was nearly twenty feet above its hardwood floors, Travis estimated. Floor-to-ceiling windows gave way to the lights of the surrounding piazza and, farther away, midtown. Reflected in the windows, he saw the glittering crowd of partygoers. Damn. He didn't get here early enough. The women wore cocktail dresses, while most of the men, like him, had gone for the black-and-white of a tuxedo. At the far end, a string quartet played "It Came Upon a Midnight Clear."

As hostess, Megan was stationed near the entry. Her low-cut, copper silk dress was fitted below her breasts, then skimmed down her legs to just above the knee. It was classy but very sexy.

"Travis, good evening." She stuck out a hand. He ignored it and kissed her cheek.

"There are a few people here who might be useful to you," she said.

"Is your dad here?" He knew a moment of doubt. What if Jonah's doctor had declared him not well enough to attend?

"He's around somewhere," Megan said. "Look, there's Sabrina." She waved to a tall, blonde woman, who came over.

Megan hugged her. "Sabrina, this is Travis Jamieson, a colleague of mine. Travis, my beautiful baby sister, Sabrina."

Sabrina was undeniably beautiful—she wouldn't have been Miss Georgia otherwise—but Travis far preferred Megan's understated appeal, the quality that made you take a second look at her and then realize you'd need a whole lot more before you figured out who this woman really was.

Travis shook Sabrina's hand. "I understand you're getting married in the New Year. Congratulations." Her convoluted relationship with Jake Warrington, now the governor of Georgia, had been front-page news.

"Thought any more about that prenup?" Megan asked.

"Yep. I thought it'd burn well on a winter's night," Sabrina said.

Megan groaned. "You are so naive. You need to protect yourself."

"Not from Jake, dummy." Sabrina turned to Travis. "Where do you stand on prenups, Travis?"

"They're for losers," he said.

"Good man." Sabrina's perfect eyebrows lifted as she glanced at her sister. "See, I'm right."

Megan shook her head. "*I'm* right, but since you guys don't do anything by the book, I guess it'll turn out okay. Sabrina and Jake have the strangest engagement," she told Travis. "They lived together when they were pretending to be engaged, but now that they're really getting married, Sabrina's living with Dad and Jake's in the governor's mansion."

"It's driving him crazy," Sabrina said with satisfaction. "But he understands—almost—that I need time to find my feet again after being swallowed up by his election campaign. It's five weeks until the wedding—by then he'll be putty in my hands."

Travis laughed at her evil grin.

"There's Cynthia." Megan pointed to a new arrival, another blonde, this one wearing a black strapless dress.

Cynthia Merritt was a lower-wattage version of Sabrina, but with diamond-sharp eyes.

"Glad you're the one organizing this bash," she said to Megan as she shook hands with Travis. "This has to be the worst job in the company."

"It hasn't been too bad," Megan said. "You look pale, are you okay?"

"Nothing a couple of years' sleep won't fix." Cynthia accepted a glass of champagne from a passing waiter, and so did Sabrina. Megan had a club soda. "And I used to think Merritt, Merritt & Finch was stressful—you should try the D.A.'s office." Cynthia pressed her fingers to her mouth. "Don't tell Dad I said that. About being stressed."

"Of course not," Megan said. "Still, you should take it easy. As Dad would say, you don't want to have a heart attack."

"Sounds quite restful," Cynthia replied, and she didn't seem to be joking. "I'll go find Dad."

Travis watched her progress, hoping she'd give him a visual lead on Jonah.

"I asked Dad to put some thought into a job for you," Megan said.

He whipped around. "You what?"

"I told him I think you're good enough to make partner at any of the top firms," Megan said.

Guilt surged through him, diluting his desire to tackle Jonah. "Let's go sit down," he suggested. He'd missed talking to her.

"I can't yet." She sipped her soda. "I need to talk to the partners, make a good impression."

That's right, her father didn't think the partners respected her. "How many partners are there?" He knew, of course, but he needed time to process the news that Megan had enrolled in his job hunt.

"Forty-one," she said. "But I'm only targeting the top ten."

"There's no Finch these days, right?"

"There hasn't been for a decade," she agreed. "Dad says some people ask if Atticus Finch ever worked here— I sometimes wonder if that's why he's kept the name."

Her cell phone rang, and she excused herself. A catering query of some kind. Megan answered a couple of questions. She ended the call and ran a hand over her face.

"Problem?" Travis asked.

"A million details that could go wrong."

"What happens if a couple of those things do go wrong?"

"They won't, I'm on top of it."

Across the room, he saw Cynthia talking to Jonah. Jonah had an arm around her shoulder and was smiling as he listened intently to her.

"Dad and Cynthia are bosom buddies." Megan had followed his glance.

Travis heard the tightness in her voice. "Megs, don't you think this is getting out of hand?"

"What?" Panic flared in her eyes. She turned in her high heels, looking for problems.

"This thing with your dad. You're killing yourself to impress him."

"What's your point?" she asked.

"Do you think it will make him give you the job?"

"It might," she said defensively.

"And even if he does…you could do everything the way he wants, but do you think he'll ever talk to you like that?" He jerked his head toward Cynthia and Jonah.

Megan paled. "That's an awful thing to say."

"Get real, Megs. You're trying to earn crumbs of love from your father, when he should love you for yourself, because you're who you are."

"Shut up."

"I hate to see you hurt."

"Then go away," she ordered, right before she obeyed her own command—she stalked off and left him.

He was about to go after her when Jonah called his name. While Travis and Megan were arguing, he'd threaded his way through the crowd.

"Megan said I should ask you why you joined PPA," he said.

"What, now?"

Jonah drew back, chin jutting; dammit, Travis couldn't offend the man again. He'd talk to Megan later, when she'd had time to calm down.

"I'd be happy to tell you," he said to Jonah, and launched into a concise version of the history he'd told Megan.

It was by anyone's standards an interesting tale. Jonah paid close attention, and at the end, he nodded. "I admire loyalty," he murmured. "So, did things work out well financially for you at PPA?"

Travis told him the growth and profitability figures he personally was responsible for. He didn't miss the gleam in Jonah's eyes.

He was describing the revenue forecasting system he'd developed when he caught sight of Megan, sitting at one of the dozens of small tables, talking to Nick Stanton. He hadn't even known Stanton was here. To his irritation, the guy was as good-looking as he'd ever been—no thinning hair or potbelly to detract from his charms. Even from here Travis could see he was smitten by Megan.

"What do you think?" Jonah asked, and Travis realized he hadn't heard the question.

Jonah repeated, "What's your view on the new corporate tax legislation?"

Travis knew enough about the law to answer while his mind was still occupied by Megan. Hadn't Nick

Stanton gotten engaged, or married? Was the guy even free to date her?

"I like your style," Jonah said. "It wouldn't hurt for you to send me your résumé." Presumably that meant he'd thrown away the one Travis sent weeks ago.

"Is this about the managing partner position?" Travis asked bluntly.

"It's the only job open," Jonah said. "You'll have some hard work to convince me you're the man for it."

"I'm not afraid of hard work." Dammit, Stanton was so close to Megan it could only be called an invasion of her personal space. So why wasn't she bawling him out the way she had Travis in the past?

"I'll send it over," Travis said, still distracted.

The friendliness of Jonah's handshake—he put his left hand over their clasped right hands as they shook—was unmistakable. Travis was in the running for the managing partner position at Merritt, Merritt & Finch.

He glanced at Megan again, at the smile she was flashing at Stanton. She wouldn't be smiling if she knew she'd paved the way for Travis to come in and steal the job she considered rightfully hers.

And that Travis would willingly steal it out from under her nose.

CHAPTER FOURTEEN

MEGAN HAD ACCEPTED Nick Stanton's offer of an escort to the buffet that was a highlight of the Christmas party, and not just because it would please her father. She would prove that she was not, as Travis had suggested, hanging around waiting for love. It made her sound pathetic. Nick Stanton was every bit the decent guy Megan's father had suggested. Polite, intelligent, with a good sense of humor. And clearly attracted to Megan. Why wouldn't she spend time with him?

"I'm so glad your dad suggested we meet," Nick said across their laden plates, almost too big for the small tables set up around the Grand Lobby.

"Me too." Megan sampled the turkey and cranberry roulade. "Mmm, this is delicious."

"Megan." Her father tapped her on the shoulder, smiling at Nick, then leaned in to add, "I need a word."

"Sure." She introduced him to Nick and the two shook hands. Jonah gave Nick a look, and the younger man took the hint. "How about I grab us a drink?" he offered.

"A chardonnay, thanks," she said.

Nick headed toward the bar.

"Didn't I tell you he was a nice guy?" Jonah asked.

"You were right."

"So were you," he said unexpectedly.

"Excuse me?"

"I had a call from Theo Hoskins this morning."

Megan's heart leaped into her mouth. "Is there a problem?"

"Not at all." Her father paused. "Since I'm still nominal head of the commercial division of Merritt, Merritt & Finch, Theo thought I was the right person to approach about giving us some of his business."

"Dad, wow, that's fantastic." Megan clutched the arms of her chair before she did something undignified, like dance around the room. Of course, Travis wouldn't think it undignified. He'd probably encourage her.

"It's a tribute to you, Megan. I admit I thought it was a long shot."

She couldn't contain an exultant laugh. "You know what I'm going to say now, don't you, Dad."

"I do," he said drily. "And the answer's yes."

She gaped. "Yes…you'll consider me to take over the firm?"

He nodded. "You're on the short list. Which seems to be getting longer by the minute," he muttered obscurely.

"Dad, thank you." She got up to kiss him.

He gave her one of the hugs that Sabrina got all the time, but which Megan suspected were more precious to her because of their rarity. "There's more news," he said.

He sounded sober; Megan sat back and scanned his face. "Are you okay?" His complexion was a little gray.

"Not as okay as I should be." Jonah sounded annoyed with himself. "I had an appointment with my cardiologist yesterday, and he's not happy with my progress."

She felt the blood drain from her face. "Are you going to have another heart attack?"

"Not if I can help it. But I do need to clear my mind of all worries, and that means letting go of Merritt, Merritt & Finch sooner than I'd planned." He pushed himself out of the chair with a grunt. "I want to announce the new managing partner before Christmas."

Barely three weeks away. Megan swallowed. That didn't leave her much time to convince her father.

Reading her mind, he said, "You'll have a formal interview for the position, just like the other candidates. But you're at the bottom of the list, my dear, I should warn you."

Momentarily, that news dampened her excitement. Then she said, "I wasn't even *on* the list five minutes ago. I can work my way up, you'll see."

Despite her concern about her father's heart, when Nick returned, she was still on a high. Conversation flowed easily. He appeared to be enjoying himself, too, the way he kept catching and holding her hand.

Her cell phone rang. She glanced at the display: unknown caller. "I'd better take this," she told Nick. "I need to keep in touch with the caterers."

"Go ahead." He squeezed her hand across the table, and his blue eyes crinkled sympathetically. What a great guy.

Megan answered the phone.

"Sit back. Stanton can see right down the front of your dress."

Her head jerked around to locate Travis. "He can not," she said automatically.

He was sitting on one of the high, black leather stools at the bar, swiveled to face her. If she could have murdered him with a look, she was certain any judge in the land would agree it was justifiable homicide.

He made the slightest gesture with his beer bottle, raising it in a toast, and said calmly, "The man's eyes are out on stalks. Unless you want him to get an eyeful of your best assets, you'd better sit back."

Megan struggled for self-possession. "These are not my best assets," she said icily. She flicked a glance at Nick, who hastily lifted his gaze from her cleavage.

"Now you've got me interested." Travis's voice changed to a purr. "Would you care to enlighten me as to which you consider the best?"

"My mind, of course." Was she insane, letting him provoke her into this discussion?

Travis chuckled. "Ah yes, and a very fine mind it is, too. But for sheer visual appeal, I'm afraid it loses out to your—"

Megan switched off the phone.

"I assume that wasn't a catering problem?" Nick asked.

"No. A colleague. A particularly irritating colleague." She forced a smile as she picked up her fork. "Now, where were we?"

Two minutes later, she decided she could excuse herself to go to the bathroom without arousing Nick's suspicions. That meant passing the bar.

"Stop it," she hissed as she neared Travis. "I don't know what you're up to, criticizing my father, and now interfering between me and Nick."

"This has nothing to do with your father." His expression was hard. "Don't you think it's a little soon to be flirting with someone else, when you and I only broke up on Monday?"

"Travis, we agreed there's nothing between us. I'm free to date whoever I want. Without being spied on."

"I still want you," he said, the words a near whisper.

Megan's mouth dried, even as she melted inside. She couldn't speak. Instead, she made her way to the bathroom. She steadied herself against the tiled wall, catching a glimpse of her flushed cheeks and bright eyes in the mirror. Splashing cold water on her face and wrists did nothing to diminish the heat.

When she walked out of the bathroom, Nick was talking to Travis.

Oh, hell.

"Megan." Nick smiled. "I just saw Travis and came over to talk. He tells me he knows you."

"*You* know Travis?" She forced a smile.

"Sure, although our paths haven't crossed for, what, thirteen years, Travis?"

Travis nodded.

"We were at Yale together," Nick said. "We were both members of the Law Journal."

Megan put a hand on the bar. She said to Travis, "I thought you graduated from Dayton."

His smile was gently mocking. "You're thinking of Kyle Prescott. He was expelled from Yale for cheating, and ended up at Dayton."

Travis was a graduate of Yale? An Ivy League lawyer, like her? Why hadn't he said?

He must have known she would be…interested.

He'd wanted her to underestimate him in the Hoskins case, she guessed, and cursed herself for assuming that his friendship with Kyle had started in Ohio. She'd let her prejudice against PPA convince her that Travis couldn't have a topflight degree.

"Excuse us, Travis," Nick said. "I'd like to introduce Megan to my father, and I see he's just managed to extricate himself from the rather gruesome death penalty debate in the corner." He held out a hand to Megan. "Coming?"

The look in Travis's dark eyes was unfathomable. She'd figured out why he hadn't told her about Yale when they first met. But later, after he'd revealed so many other details of his past...why hadn't he shared this one?

The weeks of work on this party, on the Hoskins case, on impressing her father suddenly piled up, compounded in her head until it felt as if her brain would explode.

"Megan?" Nick prompted.

She grasped his hand. "Let's go."

BARBARA HOSKINS'S custody countersuit was heard on Monday morning, so Megan spent another weekend working. That, and her anger toward Travis for judging her relationship with her father, not to mention his failure to mention he had a degree from Yale, left her on a short fuse.

Judge Potter was also low on patience. In the hearing before the Hoskinses' he'd thrown out a claim against a toy store for promoting Christmas gifts instead of "holiday gifts," and was muttering darkly about people who wasted the court's time.

Travis didn't look much happier than Megan, but he managed to disarm the judge with a quip about Santa Claus and a drunken reindeer. Then he got down to business. He laid out a compelling case for Barbara to have custody of the children. He'd obviously decided not to put Barbara on the stand, so Megan couldn't cross-examine her about the home-alone incident, which he covered in a way that made it seem like a minor slip up.

Megan didn't want Theo on the stand either, because Travis would undoubtedly dive into the alcohol issue.

Judge Potter listened intently to both arguments. Megan reminded herself he'd found in her favor the last time she'd appeared in front of him. But once again it was too close to call.

The judge went through his familiar glasses-polishing routine before he retired, then took his sweet time returning. He summarized both sides of the case, then concluded, "I award custody of Marcus Hoskins to his father, Theo Hoskins, and custody of Chelsea Hoskins to her mother, Barbara Hoskins."

Megan grabbed the edge of the table. She couldn't think of a worse verdict than splitting up the two children. They relied so heavily on each other. "Your Honor," she began, "this is unsatisfactory…"

The judge turned glacial eyes on her. "Ms. Merritt, I have announced my verdict, and I am certain you know the proper process for appeal."

She didn't want to antagonize him further, so she subsided. But as soon as the judge had left, she dragged Theo into a meeting room. She tossed her briefcase on the table and didn't bother sitting.

"You need to give up custody of Marcus," she ordered.

"Absolutely not," Theo said. "I am as upset as you that the kids are being separated, but if anyone's going to give a child up, it should be Barbara."

"Theo, you've told me yourself it's hard work

having the kids around full-time." He'd made the comment every time they'd spoken the past few days. "If you let Marcus go with Barbara, it will stand in your favor when we get a permanent custody order." There was a chance Barbara would benefit from the move, but she doubted it. "You want shared custody, don't you? Having the children with you all the time isn't your ultimate aim?" Poor kids.

"I suppose," he said sulkily.

"Then show the judge in the next round that you truly have the kids' best interests at heart. We'll put it on paper now, present it to Barbara and her lawyer, and it will go in the case records. You still have custody of Marcus, but you're choosing to let him stay with his mother."

He ran a hand over his eyes. "Fine."

She called Travis from her cell phone. "My client has a proposition." She told him the details. "Can you run it by your client?"

She ended the call aware the problem was only half solved. Finishing it off meant…she closed her eyes and tried to think of another way. *Nada.*

"Are you okay?" Theo gave her an opening.

An opening to commit professional suicide. She met his gaze, drew a last, sustaining breath, and tackled the man who could kill her hopes with one phone call to her father.

"You need help, Theo. I want you to get treatment for your alcohol dependency." She held up a hand. "I'm not interested in hearing that you don't have one—the look in your eyes every time Barbara mentions it tells me there's some kind of problem. Fix it, for your children's sake. Or you'll find that news gets out."

As threats went, the veil was gossamer thin.

Theo's jaw dropped and he ran a hand over his thinning, sandy hair. "You would tell people I'm an— I have a problem?"

"News will get out," she repeated.

He sagged back in his chair. Then sat bolt upright. Then sagged again.

"I can't...do as you ask...while the divorce is in process," he said. "It's too risky."

She knew that. She waited for him to find a solution.

He licked his lips, as if right now he was craving a drink. "How about if I promise to attend a program—" he couldn't bring himself to say anything that might incriminate him, she noticed "—the minute we're done with the divorce?"

In that moment she liked Theo more than she had before.

"That's acceptable," she said. A movement in the doorway caught her eye. Travis.

How much had he heard?

Impossible to tell from his blank expression. "I spoke to Barbara," Travis said. "We'll take the deal."

She held her breath, half-expecting him to say Barbara would file for permanent custody now that Theo had "confessed" to his problem. But he turned and walked away.

Theo wasn't the only one with a dependency, Megan realized. She might have told Travis they were finished, but every cell in her body craved him.

JONAH MERRITT HAD INVITED Travis to a formal interview at his home on Tuesday morning.

The meeting took place in Jonah's study, amid what Travis considered an excess of oak paneling.

"When you first sent me your application a few months back, I threw it straight in the trash." Jonah steepled his fingers and eyed Travis as if he was a serial killer in the dock. "If Megan hadn't told me you were representing Barbara Hoskins, I'd never have thought of you again. But that intrigued me enough to ask around."

Travis doubted anyone in Atlanta had more contacts in legal circles than Jonah. Whatever Jonah wanted to know, he would find out.

"That firm you work for is slime," Jonah said. He held up a hand as Travis protested. "Yes, yes, I commend your loyalty, and there's never been any whiff of scandal in your property division. But the fact is, you'll have trouble getting anyone to take you seriously as a partner at a firm like Merritt, Merritt & Finch."

Didn't he know it. Just last night, Travis had heard from the last of the firms he'd approached in recent months about a job, canceling the one interview he'd managed to score besides this one. He'd had high hopes, since he had a couple of clients at PPA who would follow him wherever he went, and he knew the other crowd wanted those clients. Unfortunately, one of the senior partners there was Robert Grayson. Travis's contact told him Grayson had nixed the idea of even interviewing him.

"I don't expect anything to come easy," Travis said.

"Ah, blue-collar nobility," Jonah said good-naturedly. He picked up a gold pen and jotted something on his notepad. "I can see running this firm would be a dream come true for you. But what's in it for me?"

"It's *your* dream that will benefit from having me on board," Travis said.

Jonah snorted, a heftier version of Megan's.

"You're about to lose control of a business you've nurtured from its conception," Travis said. "You're at the mercy of whoever takes over. If you're lucky, or smart, you'll choose someone who's not going to rest on your laurels, but who's going to take the firm forward."

"And that's you." Jonah pointed at Travis with his gold pen; momentarily it glowed in a ray of sunlight pouring through the sash window.

"One thing about working at Prescott Palmer, we know how to win business, and how to hold on to it," Travis said. "In my division, we have a twenty-six-percent profit margin, and we've had double-digit growth every year. Triple-digit some years."

No mistaking Jonah's interest. "I suppose you can verify all those numbers?"

"Of course." Travis leaned forward. He knew he looked too eager, but he couldn't help himself. "You might be wondering how I could ever command the respect of your staff, especially your partners. I'm afraid my strategy for that is a little crass."

Jonah frowned.

"I plan to buy their respect," Travis said. "When I tell them what bonuses I expect them to achieve and how we're going to do it, I anticipate they'll do exactly what I want until they can see if I'm telling the truth. And I always make my targets." He added, "I assume your blue-blooded lawyers are as wed to the mighty dollar as my red-blooded ones."

"They might be," Jonah conceded, "but I don't want to see Merritt, Merritt & Finch turned into the kind of money-grubbing operation you have at PPA."

"That would hardly achieve my objective of the respect of the legal fraternity," Travis said. "I'm saying there will be improvements I can make to your firm that won't detract in the slightest from its reputation. I'd be more than happy to clear them with you first."

Jonah sat back and regarded Travis through hooded eyes. "One of the key partners whose respect you'd need to earn is my daughter."

"Megan's the best lawyer I know." Travis didn't add a qualifier like *besides me* or *besides you*. Jonah acknowledged that with an amused smile. "While she may initially be surprised at my getting the job, I assure you the respect is mutual," Travis said. "I understand she recommended me to you." Which she would never have done had she known all the facts.

Jonah gave him a searching look, and Travis wondered if he would mention Megan's interest in the job. He guessed her father would protect her confidentiality, just as he would protect Travis's.

"I have to say, this is all very interesting." Jonah laced his fingers on the desk. "You've given me plenty to think about."

Travis's mind reeled. Jonah Merritt was taking him seriously.

He couldn't go another day without telling Megan the truth.

CHAPTER FIFTEEN

MEGAN WASN'T SURPRISED when Travis called and said he wanted to see her. Ever since he'd whispered that he still wanted her, the words had resonated through her. Burrowing into her emotions. Demanding satisfaction.

She assumed he felt the same.

"Come to my place for dinner," she said. It was time to tell him what was on her mind.

Silence.

"You can cook," she offered. "Just give me a shopping list."

Travis showed up in jeans and a white shirt, open at the neck. He looked tan even in winter. Megan's clingy grape-colored cashmere sweater and black velvet skirt were much dressier…but that was the least of their differences.

She almost got cold feet. Then, boldly, she went up on tiptoe to kiss him on the mouth. After the briefest hesitation, he responded. She sensed he was still holding back, and it made her tremble. Later, she would do her damnedest to unleash his passion.

Travis followed her into the cream-carpeted living and dining area that opened to a slate-floored kitchen. "Classy," he said.

"It's not as homey as your place," Megan admitted.

"But it's handy to Dad's and in daylight it has great views over Chastain Park." The apartment was also a decent size, thanks to her substantial partner's salary at Merritt, Merritt & Finch.

"*Classy* wasn't an insult," he said, amused. He caught sight of her Christmas tree, a puny, artificial number next to the TV she seldom watched. "That, however, is a disgrace."

"I'm never here," she protested. "I'd be forever sweeping up pine needles without having time to enjoy the tree. I have Christmas at Dad's place and he has a real one." Supplied and decorated by a professional, unlike Travis's.

She led him into the kitchen. "I bought all the food, even the tamarind pulp, though I have no idea what it is. It looks like hundred-year-old Jell-O."

"It softens up when you know what to do with it," he said. Their gazes met.

After a long moment, Travis turned to the counter. "Point me at your knives, and I'll get started."

While she watched, he prepared a Thai chicken curry, fragrant with cilantro, basil and coconut, and served it on steamed rice. He seemed quiet, reflective…or maybe that was her.

"This smells amazing," Megan said, as she sat down at right angles to him at her polished oak dining table.

He dug into his meal.

"Don't you like it?" he asked, when he realized she was just pushing the food around the plate.

"It's lovely." She took another of those deep breaths that had served her so well with Theo the other day. "But it's not what I want."

As always, he was on her wavelength. His eyes

darkened and he pushed his plate away. Extended a hand to her. A minute later, they were ensconced on the couch in her living room.

Travis leaned forward, elbows on his knees, hands clasped. "I said I wanted to talk to you."

"We talk too much," Megan said.

He lifted his head. "Excuse me?"

"All talking does is raise our differences." She shifted so she was slightly angled to him. "I'm sick of talking about kids and careers and families. Can't we just forget about the future and do…this?"

She put her hand on his knee.

He jerked back into the cushions.

"Megs," he said, "I wish it was that simple."

"It can be." Megan ran her fingers over the length of his thigh. Travis groaned. "I care about you," she said, as honest as she dared. "I care a lot. I want to show you how much, even if it's just once."

She continued her journey up over his hip to his waist. She tugged his T-shirt out of his jeans and pressed her palm to his stomach.

"You're…going to have to stop that." The words came out uneven, through a dragging breath.

Reveling in the effect she had on him, she slid her hand across his abdomen. "If you want me to stop, you'll have to make me."

He clamped her hand firmly in place.

"Dammit, Megan," Travis said hoarsely. He hauled her into his lap. This was new, this bold ardor of hers, and he was only human. He shoved aside the guilt and concentrated all his senses on the woman in his arms.

Megan might have started the kiss, but Travis took control. His hand in her hair, he tugged her head back and deepened the kiss. He cupped her butt possessively, drawing her against him.

Releasing her mouth, he rained kisses over her face, then down her neck to the base of her throat, where he licked and caressed that tender spot. Megan curled her fingers into his hair and groaned. "Please," she half gasped, half sobbed. "Travis, *please*."

"What is it, Megs?" he said raggedly.

She reached a finger to trace his mouth. "Tonight. Just tonight."

There was nothing he wanted more.

But *tonight* was meant to be about telling Megan he'd applied for the top job at Merritt, Merritt & Finch. That through some miracle—or more precisely, thanks to her intervention—he'd found his way onto the short list. Which meant he might, just might, end up her boss.

He ran his thumbs down her cheeks to the corners of her mouth and couldn't think of a way to say it that didn't sound seedy. Dishonest. His throat seized up like a rusty latch, and not one damn word could get out.

"Megan," he managed to say at last, "I can't begin to tell you how much I want you. Not to mention I like you, I like being with you." Her gaze flickered at the lukewarm sentiment; he pressed on. "But I can't make love to you without putting everything on the table."

To his surprise, her hands fisted, drummed against his chest. "Those things that could come between us…they don't matter, Travis. Not when we're only talking one night. My father told me something tonight that makes a relationship between you and me even more of an impossibility. I want to make love with you before everything gets even more complicated."

He covered her hands with his. "You *know?*" And she still wanted to make love?

She blinked. "Like I said, Dad told me." She stared at him. "How do *you* know?"

"From your father."

She groaned and smacked his chest.

"Ouch." Travis laced his fingers through hers, left them splayed on his skin. "What was that for?"

"I can't believe Dad even mentioned it to you," she said. "He had no right."

In that moment, he realized they were talking at cross-purposes.

He slid her off his lap, back onto the couch. "What exactly did your father tell you?"

"That I'm on the short list for head of Merritt, Merritt & Finch." She jumped up. "Now that you know...I have champagne in the fridge."

He pulled her back down. "Jonah told *you* you're on the short list?"

"At the bottom of the list," she admitted. "But I'll change that."

"Where does making love fit in?"

She colored. "Travis, I care about you. I—I'm desperate to make love to you. But I can't see how we can have a proper relationship."

"Because you're so hung up on your damn career," he snapped.

"Because you won't accept that a woman may not want kids."

They stared at each other, breathing heavily. Stalemate.

Her breasts rose and fell beneath that delectably soft sweater. Travis could discern the outline of her bra, and just that chaste sight set him on fire. One night with her would never be enough. More than one night would lead to disaster.

"You know I need to get my life back on track," he told her. "I don't want to make the same mistake with a woman that I made with my job."

"You're calling me the female equivalent of PPA," she said after a moment. "Don't you care about me at all?"

She'd said she cared about him. A lot. What did that mean? Travis felt an odd ache in his chest.

"It would be a mistake," he reiterated.

She drew in a sharp breath, destroying any hope that she might not have noticed he hadn't answered the question.

"You're just like my father," she said slowly.

His chin jerked back. "What's that supposed to mean?"

"I thought—" she pressed her hands to her cheeks "—I thought you saw me for myself. Wanted *me*."

"I did." *I do.*

She shook her head. "You were right about Dad— I've always been afraid that something I do, or don't do, will stop him loving me."

He cursed.

"You're the same," she said. "You've made a decision to withhold love from any woman who won't buy into your perfect family life."

"That's not true," he snapped.

"I can't believe I nearly…" She wiped her eyes. "Do you know, I was even wondering if we could *compromise?*"

His heart leaped. She'd thought that far?

"I can't," she said, on a note of revelation. "I won't. I won't love someone whose love is conditional on me being a certain kind of person."

"I don't—" He stopped. Why even have this conversation, when love wasn't part of the equation. He looked around the room for an escape and saw that scrawny, plastic excuse for a Christmas tree. A sign? He needed a woman who would embrace family, build something lasting, something of real worth, with him…and their children.

"I've already loved like that, Travis," she whispered. "I know how much it hurts. Never again."

He left her sitting on the couch, arms wrapped around herself as if hers was the only love she could depend on. Her cheeks were pale but dry, although her eyes were suspiciously moist.

It wasn't until he was in his own house, climbing into bed alone, that Travis realized he hadn't told Megan he was on the short list.

CHAPTER SIXTEEN

MEGAN WALKED into Merritt, Merritt & Finch on Wednesday morning with her head held high and her spirits crushed. She had offered Travis pretty much everything short of her undying devotion and he'd thrown it back at her. Thank goodness she hadn't been stupid enough to fall in love with him, because if this was how it felt to be rejected by a guy she *cared about*...

She rubbed her chest, then stopped when she saw Trisha watching. "Dig out a copy of the Hoskins prenup," she ordered. Trisha raised her eyebrows at the peremptory tone. Too bad. Megan needed to hammer Barbara Hoskins in the divorce, and the prenup was her weapon of choice.

She stalked into her office. Travis had never been in here, so memories of him didn't follow her around the way they did at home or in one of the meeting rooms. She unzipped her laptop case and set the computer on her limed Scandinavian oak desk. As she plugged in the power cord, she caught sight of a paperback book, its colorful cover incongruous among the legal tomes on her bookshelf.

Travis's mystery novel, *Silence in the Tomb*. He'd suggested she'd enjoy it. She pulled the book from the shelf and opened it near the middle as she sank into her crimson, wool-upholstered chair.

Ugh, some man was being bludgeoned to death. By a woman scorned. Megan's interest picked up, and she read a couple of pages. When her desk phone rang, she shut the book with a guilty snap.

"There's a man here to see you," the floor receptionist said, "and he's carrying flowers."

Travis! Could he have missed her as much as she'd missed him after he'd left? Could he have realized the mistake was in leaving, not in staying? Maybe she wouldn't have to bludgeon him to death, after all. "Send him in," she said. The moment she hung up, she wished she'd asked for a minute so she could check her appearance.

She was still patting her hair when her office door opened…to admit Nick Stanton, carrying an enormous bouquet of roses.

"Nick." She caught herself just in time, put a lift in her voice. Smiled as she walked around the desk.

"I've been calling," he said, "and not getting through. I thought you might need personal persuasion to a dinner date."

"I'm sorry, it's been crazy around here."

His gaze went to the novel in her hand. Megan tossed it in the trash. She took the proffered flowers and inhaled their perfume. "These are beautiful, thank you."

"Beautiful enough for a date?" His blue eyes crinkled in that charming way he had. "I had a great time the other night."

She set the flowers down on her desk. "Me, too." Until Travis turned up and eclipsed Nick and every other man in the room.

But Nick was much more her usual kind of guy, with the bonus of being funny and interesting. And he liked her.

She noticed him casting an appreciative look down her legs, lengthened by her above-the-knee skirt and high heels. And when he looked back at her face, his smile widened.

Maybe that was what she needed... A reminder that Travis Jamieson wasn't the only man in the world. "I'd love to have dinner." She forced the words past the lump in her throat.

"Wonderful." Impulsively, he took her hands. "Name the day."

It was so nice to have an uncomplicated guy so openly interested in her. She was a hundred percent sure he wasn't about to spring on her that she had to give up work and have his babies. Or...

"You're not after a job at Merritt, Merritt & Finch, are you?" she asked in sudden suspicion.

His laugh was puzzled. "I'm working for my dad, like you."

Of course he was.

"How about Saturday?" she said. "Barring any unexpected developments in the divorce case I'm handling." She grimaced. "My work does take up a lot of my time, Nick."

"As it would," he said cheerfully. "You're busier than I am at the moment, so I'll fit in around you."

What a guy.

TRAVIS THUMBED the elevator button for Megan's floor. He might have made a royal mess of this whole thing, but he had to be honest with her right now. Nothing would stop him.

Not that it would achieve anything, beyond a clearing of his conscience. And a lessening of her shock if he did happen to get that job…

"Travis Jamieson to see Megan Merritt," he told the third-floor receptionist.

"Do you have an appointment?"

"No, I—" He heard her laughter somewhere beyond the woman. Not loud, but because it was Megan's laugh, Travis heard it. It came from the glass-walled corner office.

It took him a moment to focus through the vertical blinds that partially screened the office. Then he stiffened. He could see Megan standing close—too close— to a man who was grinning at something she'd said. A man who just happened to be *holding her hands*.

Travis took the phone the receptionist had picked up and put it back on its cradle, ignoring her protest. "I'll announce myself." He strode to the office and threw open the door. "What the hell's going on?"

Megan jerked back from Nick, who'd just been telling her how much he liked her eyes. Her heart pounded at the sight of Travis.

"Sorry, Megan." Anna, the receptionist burst in behind him. "He walked right past me."

Nick let go of her hands, but he took his time about it. "Hey, Travis," he said pleasantly, but with a hint of steel that suggested he found it more than coincidental that Travis had twice showed up in the same place as Megan.

"What are you doing here?" Travis's gaze traveled to the roses. "Don't answer that."

"I had no intention of answering," Nick said. "What are *you* doing here?"

"He's here about the divorce case we're both

working," Megan said. She caught Travis's barely perceptible shake of the head. He wasn't here on business. This was all personal.

Nick's head swiveled from one to the other, clearly dubious. She wanted to tell him she'd see him on Saturday...but if Travis was here because he'd reconsidered... "Nick, I need to get to work," she said. "I'll call you later to finalize those details."

Nick wasn't thrilled. But he was a gentleman, so with a squeeze of her hand, he departed, along with the receptionist.

In their wake was a heavy, throbbing silence. And fury in Travis's gorgeous dark eyes.

He's here! He couldn't leave me! There was no mistaking his reaction to Nick—jealousy, pure and simple.

She was still mad at him, but maybe, because no matter what he'd said last night, he was here now, she could meet him halfway. She sucked in a breath that steadied her nerves, then grabbed his arms. "Travis, just now, with Nick, it was nothing. I promise."

She stepped closer until she was pressed against him. She felt his heart speed up and sighed with satisfaction. "I'm so glad you're here."

His chin jerked back, as if she'd landed an uppercut. "Megan, *I'm* sorry. I had no right to act so possessive just now. No claim over you." He stepped away and released her with a deliberateness that sent a chill through the room.

"Tell me what this is about," she said. "I told you how I felt about you last night, and I'm still feeling stupid. Did I just make a fool of myself again?"

"That job you want," he said. "Running Merritt, Merritt & Finch."

"What about it?"

"I want it, too."

"You mean…you want me to have it?" She scanned his face in bewilderment. Was he saying he wanted her to stick with her career?

He clenched his jaw. "I *don't* want you to have it. Megan, before I ever met you, I sent my résumé to your father…"

He went on to tell her things she'd never guessed. Unbelievable things about a goal of running Merritt, Merritt & Finch. About how as soon as he'd heard Megan was representing Theo, he'd pursued Barbara. About meetings with her father she knew nothing about. "Yesterday, Jonah agreed to consider my application."

"To—to head up Merritt, Merritt & Finch?" She stumbled on the words, groped behind her for the edge of her desk. "I'm up against *you?*"

"And several other candidates who are favored over us," he said.

The pieces fell into place in Megan's head, more slowly than they should have. "All this time you've been trying to get to my father."

He nodded.

Words and images bombarded her. Travis watching her in The Jury Room—except, obviously, his focus had been her father. The basketball game, where he'd guessed her ambition. His questions about her career goals and her personal life; winning her sympathy with his story about his family and his desire to restore his town's pride in him; letting her introduce him to her father, letting her urge Jonah to see him as partner material; his kisses; his refusal to make love to her…

She felt a peculiar emptiness somewhere deep inside her.

Megan teetered dangerously on her heels; Travis's traitorous hands reached to steady her. Evading his grasp became her sole mission. Sheer willpower stiffened her spine, enabled her to put one foot in front of the other and walk to the door of her office. Which she opened.

"Out." The word emerged not far above a whisper.

Travis didn't move. When had he ever done anything that didn't suit him? "I should have told you sooner," he said. "I didn't realize how complicated things would get between us. I'm sorry."

All this time—*all this time*—he'd been deceiving her. Megan knew the full impact of what he'd done would hit later, after he was gone.

Travis cursed. "Stop looking as if I've drowned your kitten. Until yesterday, I wasn't even on the radar for this job, and neither were you. No matter what either of us wanted."

"But you knew you wanted it, and you didn't tell me."

"I'm telling you now. I'm sorry."

"Sorry enough to withdraw your application?" she snapped.

He hesitated, his jaw tense. "This is my chance to make my parents proud, my hometown proud. You told me yourself, you're last on your dad's list. What's the point of me pulling out, just to give someone like Grayson a better chance?"

"That's what you had against Robert." She clutched her head. "I thought you were jealous."

"I *was* jealous. And worried about you."

She snorted. "Why are you still here?"

"I have no idea." He headed for the door, stopped right in front of her, so close she could see twin lines of strain etched at the corners of his mouth.

"Good luck with the job, Megan," he said.

TRAVIS WAS DEPRESSED—and reluctantly *im*pressed—by Megan's ability to be in a meeting with him, yet not be in it. Twice during the week that followed his revelation, they had meetings with the Hoskinses. Travis couldn't take his eyes off her, couldn't block out her melodious voice, imagined he could smell the scent of her clear across the room. And, dammit, not just when they were in the same room. All day, every day. All night, every night.

But Megan was a consummate professional, shaking his hand with no more emotion than she showed toward his client. Her face, always so easy for him to read, was calm and blank.

He sat in his office late on Thursday night, rereading the Hoskins prenup for what felt like the hundredth time, and admitted she was driving him nuts.

To make matters worse, despite their studied politeness, the tension between him and Megan was affecting their work—progress had stalled on the Hoskins negotiations. Jonah wanted to make a decision by Christmas; he wouldn't be impressed with either of them over this delay. Plus, if they didn't break through before Christmas, they'd be in court in the New Year, airing the Hoskinses' dirty laundry to the world. Travis didn't want to do that to his client, and he had to assume Megan didn't want it, either.

He didn't know for sure, because she wouldn't take

his calls. They were communicating via cool, formal e-mail—at least, hers were cool and formal, starting *Dear Mr. Jamieson*—and through her assistant phoning his assistant.

On one front, at least, things were going well. Travis had had another meeting with Jonah, where he'd talked through his ideas for the firm. Jonah had asked the kind of questions Travis excelled at. He'd managed not to rush his replies, taken time to lay out the pros and cons. Jonah had interjected, questioned…and approved, judging by his short, sharp nods. Travis had seen that nod before; Megan had the exact same mannerism.

Dammit, could she please butt out of his mind? Apparently not. He found himself remembering her humiliation, her shock, her sense of betrayal.

How had his attempt to restore his integrity ended in him violating the trust of a woman he…cared for?

What a damn mess.

Travis fanned the pages of the prenup, a testament to one couple's lack of faith in their own future. How many times had he lectured Megan about the importance of working at a relationship? He dropped the prenup in the trash.

He might have blown it with Megan as far as their personal relationship was concerned—he didn't even want to think about the gut-ache that gave him—but if he was going to be able to live with himself, there was only one thing he could do. He wasn't sure how, but he had to give her every chance to get that job.

AT SEVEN THE NEXT MORNING, Travis called Megan's direct office line from his home. He withheld his number, in case she had caller ID and wouldn't pick up from him. He stood next to the kitchen counter, too nervous to sit on one of the bar stools.

"Megan Merritt, hello?" She sounded tired, as if she'd just got in and hadn't yet had her first cup of that damned espresso she drank to impress her father.

A nervous sweat broke out on Travis's forehead. He visualized her sitting at her desk, bitter brew in hand, brushing a strand of honey-blond hair back behind her ear, maybe smothering a yawn. He wanted to be with her.

"Hello?" she repeated.

"It's me," he said, his words rough. "I can't tell you how good it is to hear you when you're not talking in that damn polite, blue-chip lawyer voice."

Silence. Then, coldly, "Excuse me, who is this?"

For a split second Travis thought she hadn't recognized him, and it hurt. Then he discerned the anger behind the coldness and couldn't quell a grin. "Very good," he said. "You had me going. No wonder I've missed you."

Each lightly uttered phrase pierced Megan with fresh pain.

It had taken days for the full scale of Travis's deception to sink in. Almost every hour, it seemed, she thought of a fresh humiliation, found one more thing she'd said or done that must have had him either laughing at her or pitying her.

She was ashamed that none of those recollections stopped her from missing his company, his conversation…his kisses. But she wasn't stupid enough to expose herself to more hurt. She glanced at the window, where a few weeks ago he'd waited in the street for her. "I have nothing to say to you, Travis."

"Too bad. I have plenty to say to you. For the good of our clients, we need to get together."

"Maybe you should have thought of our clients' welfare before you offered to represent Barbara with your ulterior motive. Or before you started kissing me, and—and stalking me and acting as if you *liked* me." Her voice too high, she clamped down on the stream of words that threatened to dissolve into tears.

"I like you," he said. "I care about you a lot." He'd matched what she felt for him. Whatever that was.

"People who care about each other don't lie and string each other along. And now, because of what you did, we're up against a brick wall in this prenup negotiation, and if Theo backs down on what he said to Dad about giving us his business, I won't—" She screeched to a halt.

Hadn't she learned by now that telling him things about herself and the firm only gave him ammunition to use against her?

Travis hadn't hesitated to take advantage of her offer to introduce him to her dad. *He didn't hesitate to defend me against Dad, either, the first time they met.* She shied away from the thought. So what if, just once, his protective instincts had got the better of his ambition?

"I can come and see you right now, and we can talk," he said.

She looked at her watch, unnecessary since she didn't have any appointments for at least an hour. "Whatever you have to say, tell me now. You have two minutes."

"I need more."

"You think I'll be harder to fool this time around?"

She heard someone arriving in the outer office and lowered her voice.

He made an exasperated sound in his throat. "We need time to get ourselves into a state where our personal antipathy doesn't rub off on Theo and Barbara. Have dinner with me tomorrow."

When she hesitated, Travis thought good sense had won through. That although Megan was still mad, she would attempt to mend their fences for the sake of their clients. His pulse sped up at the thought of dinner with her and his mind raced ahead to how he would fix this. Once he got her to the restaurant, he would explain how he planned to help her. If he told her over the phone, she wouldn't believe him.

"I can't. I have a date."

Travis felt as if the wind had been punched out of him. From somewhere he dragged a breath that hurt his lungs. "Who with?" He didn't recognize his own voice.

"With Nick, of course." Another pause. "I've seen him a couple of times the past week. I *trust* him."

Travis paced to the kitchen window. He looked out over the street and counted to ten as he watched the progress of the newspaper boy on his bike. Okay, so she was dating Nick. She'd dated Robert Grayson, too, and he hadn't meant anything to her. Of course, Grayson was nowhere near as eligible as Stanton, who was probably every girl lawyer's dream.

He had to ask. "Are you sleeping with him?"

She let out a hiss. "That's none of your business."

Her hostility gave him no clues as to the real answer.

"Okay then," he said, "would you say he's your boyfriend?"

He expected her to repeat the none-of-your-business

mantra, leaving him to flip-flop between hope and a despair that was such unfamiliar territory, he could have been walking on Mars.

"He's getting that way," Megan said, and Travis was shocked. For a woman he'd never slept with, never even got close to naked with, she packed a mighty wallop.

"Travis?"

"Yes?" Could this get any worse?

"Your two minutes are up."

Apparently, it could.

CHAPTER SEVENTEEN

MEGAN HUNG UP the phone while she was still capable of coherent speech. It rang again immediately; still dazed from the shock of talking to Travis, she answered it.

"I just realized what you meant when you mentioned Theo talking to your father," Travis said. "He's giving Merritt, Merritt & Finch some of his business, right?"

She hesitated, then figured he would hear it on the grapevine soon enough. "Theo's transferred about five percent of his business to us." Five percent was a significant amount with Atlanta's largest property development company.

"With the promise of more," Travis guessed.

She said nothing.

"So now you're worried—" his confidence seemed to grow with each word "—that Theo will pull out of that if Barbara digs her heels in over the prenup. And if Theo reneges, your father will scratch you from his short list."

She closed her eyes. "Go away."

"There has to be a way around this," he mused.

"I'm sure when you figure it out you can use it to your advantage," she snapped.

"I can't do it on my own. We need to brainstorm." He sounded as if he was sitting straighter; his voice was sharper. "You and I will spend the weekend at my place. We're going to crack this."

"Are you insane? I'm not going anywhere near your place to help you steal my job."

"Megs," he said, and her stomach tied itself in knots, "if you want this job, you have until Christmas to convince your dad. That's one week. We're not going to get this case finished, and you in Theo's good books, unless we team up. Barbara's just as keen for us to get this over with fast."

"Obviously you think this will help you," she said, "so why should I agree?"

"It won't help me. And you don't have a better idea."

"You're blackmailing me," she said, aware she was being melodramatic. Aware too, that she was at the end of her tether.

"Whatever it takes," he said, sounding way more cheerful than he had any right to be. "By the way, we're going to be very busy. Better cancel that date with Nick."

Jerk. "That's fine," she lied, "I'll be seeing Nick on Christmas Day anyway."

She took grim satisfaction when Travis hung up without another word.

MEGAN FIGURED that if her future depended on getting Theo's business, and if winning the battle of the prenup was key to that, she would put everything into it. The way she always did. Which meant working with Travis.

And accepting the need to see Travis at seven in the morning, the time they'd agreed to start work on

Saturday. He was right. They couldn't work at her office or his, not without attracting attention to the unconventional way they were handling this case.

Normally, the lawyers and their clients would have meeting after meeting, both sides giving a little each time until an end was reached. Much the way they'd been doing with the Hoskinses so far. Now, she and Travis planned to short-circuit the process by getting to the end point themselves, and presenting it to their respective clients.

She figured they couldn't do any worse than they were with the Hoskinses involved. All she had to do was survive a weekend of working with Travis. Which she could do, as a professional.

Travis led her to the dining room, where he had files and papers spread out on the craftsman-style table. "I've made a list of the outstanding issues, and some possible solutions." He ushered her into a seat.

She opened her briefcase. "Me, too."

"So all we have to do," he said, "is work through every possible permutation."

"Uh-huh." She tried not to notice he hadn't shaved yet. "Theo's starting point is that Barbara signed a prenup and he doesn't have to give an inch."

"I'm sure it is," Travis said drily. "Luckily for Barbara, we're living in the real world."

"Lucky that she gets to try and bleed Theo dry?"

"We're not in the courtroom now, Counselor. You know Barbara has a legitimate claim."

Megan plugged in her laptop. "It's going to be a long weekend."

"I have a guest room," he said.

"I'm not sleeping here," she spit.

He held up a hand for a truce. "Let's just get this done."

With her knuckles, Megan traced the frown line that had taken up permanent residence in her forehead. "Why are you doing this, Travis? I know we both need the divorce resolved, but by speeding this up, you're giving me a chance to bring Theo's business over to Merritt, Merritt & Finch. You're shooting yourself in the foot." She'd thought about it half the night, and couldn't see where he was going to get his advantage.

"It's a risk I'm willing to take. There's no guarantee your dad will give you the job, even if Theo hands you every last cent of his legal business." He shifted a stack of papers to make way for hers. "Besides, Theo's account will be a nice revenue stream when I'm running the firm."

She butted her papers up against his. "You think you're a better candidate than I am."

"In some ways. Not in others." He slid a jar of pens toward her. "Put my help down to a guilty conscience."

"Who'd have thought you could work at PPA this long and still have a conscience?" It was a low blow, but it made her feel better.

His expression cooled. "Put it down to my preference for a fair fight, then."

That, she could more readily believe. "It's not a fair fight when I only just found out you're in it."

"Like I told you," he said, "I didn't think it would come down to this, you and me, head-to-head. If your dad had kept you off the list, and I'd somehow managed to convince him to put me on it, the worst that would have happened was that I'd end up your boss."

Her fingers curled on the tabletop.

"Will you stay as head of the family division if I get that job?" he asked.

She forced her fingers flat. "You think I'd let you drive me out of my own family's business? You're over-estimating your own importance."

"Ouch," he said mildly.

"I'd stay, if only to make your life a misery," she promised.

A glint lit his eyes. "You couldn't do that, Megs. Even when we argue, you're more fun than a runaway roller coaster."

Damn him. She ducked her face, and her swimming gaze gradually focused in on a spreadsheet. "Let's talk numbers," she said.

Travis snapped into business mode, which helped her forget he was wearing faded jeans and a soft plaid shirt that on some men might have looked like something his father would wear, but on Travis looked un-utterably cool. If he were to stroll down Fifth Avenue in New York right now, the stores would be full of ancient plaid shirts tomorrow.

After they'd agreed which clauses of the prenup were most contentious, they each took time out to make notes and consider their options. Travis poured apple juice and set banana muffins on the table. Megan realized she was starving; she broke a still-warm muffin open and ate while she worked.

An hour later, Travis broke her concentration. "You done there?" He indicated her notes.

"Yep." The time had been incredibly productive, much more than sitting in her office with all kinds of interruptions, even on a weekend.

"I'll show you mine if you'll show me yours," Travis quipped.

She pretended the innuendo had bypassed her, and shoved her notes across the table.

TRAVIS GAVE HER what he'd done, then he read through Megan's notes. Some of her claims were laugh-out-loud outrageous, other demands were more reasonable.

He eyed her, engrossed in reading his work. She gave a soft snort—he figured she was up to the part about Barbara being deprived of sufficient time to understand the prenup. Her honey-colored hair was pulled back off her face, showing the hint of a widow's peak, and her light floral perfume, combined with the aroma of Costa Rican coffee, captivated him.

"You must be dreaming." She tapped the total dollar amount at the bottom of the page with her pen.

He *was* dreaming, but not about this divorce settlement. "Okay, slugger," he said, focusing in on the facts, "if you can do better, give me your best shot."

They talked all day, until they were both hoarse, gulping water, then returning to the fray.

The verbal dance was challenging, exhilarating. For every point Travis conceded to Megan, he forced her to give one right back.

By five o'clock, Travis thought the kinks in his back might be permanent. He stood and stretched, felt the crack of bones and joints. "I'm impressed with us," he said. "We've done a lot."

Megan leaned back in her seat, her arms hanging loose at her sides, her fingers waggling in what he took to be some kind of exercise. "If we can get this done by Christmas, it'll be a happier holiday for Marcus and Chelsea," she said.

"Yeah. Once Barbara and Theo are done fighting over money, they might find some time for the kids." One hand behind his neck, he grasped his elbow with the other hand and pulled back until he felt a welcome stretch in his tricep. "For someone who doesn't want kids, you sure take a personal interest in Chelsea and Marcus."

She shot him a look. "It's not about kids anymore, Travis, me and you."

"It's not about some cockeyed idea about someone—" *him* "—not loving you the right kind of way, either."

She held an asset list high in front of her face and pretended to read.

"Here's a question." With one finger, he tweaked the top of the page so he could see her eyes. "When did Theo give Merritt, Merritt & Finch that five percent?"

She twitched the paper, but he didn't let go. "Dad told me about it at the Christmas party."

"I figured. So here's what I know about you and your career and kids." He was thinking out loud. "When you told Theo to get himself to rehab or else you'd tell the world he's an alcoholic—"

She gasped. "I never said that."

"Not in so many words," he said with satisfaction and something curiously like pride. "But you threatened your client when he was in a position to take that business away from you."

She swallowed. "I wasn't sure you heard."

"It's not like I'm going to report you to anyone, Megs." She flinched at the nickname. "Fact is, you risked your all-fired important career to make sure those kids ended up with a sober dad."

She blinked. "So what are you saying…that I'm less set in my ways than you are?"

"No." Hell, maybe he *was* saying that. He let go of her page and slumped back in his seat. "I'm saying you don't know what you want. Just like your damned coffee."

"Luckily," she said, "I do know what I *don't* want. And that's a self-centered man like you." She looked down her nose at him. "I suggest you get back to work."

His thoughts swirled in all directions, no way could he concentrate on legalese. He pulled out his cell. "I'll order us a pizza."

"You're not going to cook?"

There was a moment's charged silence as they thought about the last time he'd cooked for her. "Pizza," he said.

They worked another couple of hours, until seven, eating pepperoni and mushroom pizza as they talked about appreciation of assets. By now the settlement agreement was taking shape. Megan and Travis were still arguing every point of the prenup, but at least it was honest argument. They knew where they stood.

"If I ever get married, I'll do a darned sight better job on my prenup than the Hoskinses did." Megan stretched her arms, lifting her sweater a tantalizing inch or two so that Travis glimpsed her midriff. He'd touched her there—was it only a week ago?—and he couldn't stop thinking about doing it again.

"Did it occur to you that if the Hoskinses had a little more faith in their marriage, with no prenup to fall back on, they might not be getting divorced?" he asked.

"Chicken and egg," she said dismissively.

"Just chicken," he corrected her.

"Excuse me?"

"People have prenuptial agreements drawn up because they're afraid the marriage won't work. So they don't commit fully, they leave themselves an exit."

"Not having a prenup might be romantic," she said. "But it overlooks the fact that people are flawed."

"So if no marriage is perfect, why insure against it going bad by signing a prenup? You need to say from the start it's going to be damned difficult but you're sticking with it no matter what."

"Spoken like a man with happily married parents," she said.

"I'm not belittling what you went through with your parents' divorce." He touched the back of her hand. She twitched but didn't pull back.

"Mom and Dad had a prenup," she said, "but the agreement didn't wreck their marriage. They were just plain wrong for each other, permanently fighting their own civil war."

"You wouldn't remember the breakup, though," he prompted.

She shook her head. "But I remember living with Cynthia and Mom, and Dad living with Daisy, his second wife, and Sabrina. Dad was so happy with Daisy, but anything to do with alimony, or his and Mom's joint custody of me and Cyn…it was a nightmare."

Her fingers were long and slim, the nails painted a pale pink that somehow tugged at his heart. Travis held his breath as he spread his fingers so his hand entirely covered hers. He hadn't been this cautious since he was sixteen and trying to sneak up on his girlfriend's hand in the movies. Megan glanced down, but she was too distracted to register his advance.

"Mom died when I was seven," she said. "She had an aneurysm, one of those things no one saw coming."

"I'm sorry, Megs." He laced his fingers through hers.

"Cynthia and I went to live with Dad and his new family full-time, not just every second weekend."

"That must have been tough."

Her eyes were unfocused. Or rather, focused on something he couldn't see. "It was surprisingly easy. Daisy was so kind and loving, and she and Dad were happy. Sabrina was like a doll for me and Cynthia to play with."

"Still, you must have felt strange," he persisted. Because her relationship with her father suggested she still had something to prove.

"When I was ten, I overhead Dad and Daisy talking about his first marriage. Turned out he and my mom were separated, about to divorce, when Mom discovered she was pregnant with me."

"So they got back together."

"Yep." She tore a little strip off the napkin she'd used with her pizza. "I see enough unhappy kids in my job to know it's sometimes worth parents staying together for the sake of their kids…as long they're willing to make an effort. No point if you're just providing a battleground for a home."

He felt a spurt of anger toward Jonah, of tenderness toward Megan, who'd had to prove herself every step of the way. "It's not your fault your parents stayed together and were miserable."

"I know that." She tapped her head to show where

she knew it. Implying her heart thought differently. "Just like I know Dad loves me, in his way. But I think," she said in a rush, "subconsciously he associates me with an unhappy period in his life, and he can't entirely forget that, and it's a barrier between us." She must have seen the shock on Travis's face, because she said, "I don't sit around worrying about this, it's just a—"

Travis surged across the table and planted his mouth on hers. Tried to tell Megan with his kiss that no one in their right mind could blame her for their unhappiness, that she was beautiful and lovable, the kind of woman who could only give a guy the best kind of thoughts.

She stiffened…then melted against him in a capitulation as complete as it was unexpected, her mouth opening to him, taking what he offered. Travis ran his fingers through the honeyed silk of her hair, then cupped the back of her head as he deepened the kiss.

Megan tensed, then shoved Travis's chest. "Stop."

When he released her, she got up from the table, her breathing uneven, her body shaking. "What was that, a pity kiss?"

"The only person I feel sorry for right now is me," he said, his eyes still on her lips.

"How could you do that after…everything?"

"You know I care about you."

"What does that mean?" she demanded.

"Uh…" He froze. "What did it mean when you said it?"

She threw her hands in the air. "Are you trying to say you love me, in your own limited way?"

He decided not to tackle the insult part of that. "Maybe I am."

"You *lied* to me." Her voice rose, and he wondered if she'd ever forget what he'd done.

"I'm trying to get you this job!"

She rubbed her face with her hands. Tired, like he was. "So you say." She let out a long breath. "If this is love…give me your best offer, Travis."

"What do you mean?" But he was afraid he knew.

"You have a plan for your life. I don't fit. Something's got to give. What will it be? Me, or your picture-perfect life?"

"You're the one who said you don't gamble," he said defensively.

"That's it," she said. "I already have your best offer."

He nodded. Fixed his gaze on the wall behind her because there was something in his eyes that threatened to make them water.

She stared at him for a long time. Travis reached out to touch her hair and broke the spell. She jerked away. "Not good enough, Travis."

CHAPTER EIGHTEEN

WITH NOTHING LEFT TO SAY about their personal relationship, Megan and Travis fell into a semisilent routine, talking only when they needed to about the prenup, drafting and redrafting clauses for the divorce settlement. When the phone rang an hour later, Megan jumped.

Travis answered it. "Hi, Dad. How's—" He stopped, and Megan heard an indistinct outpouring from the phone. Travis cursed, and she set down her pen. There was a problem, a big one, going by his increasingly black expression.

He glanced at his watch. "Of course I'll go. I'll leave now, and keep you posted." He ended the call and cursed again. "It's Gina," he said to Megan. "She and Scott have run off to get married."

Megan squawked "When? Where?"

"It's my fault. She called the night of your firm's party and I told her I'd call her back. She said Scott had proposed." He banged the heel of his hand against his forehead.

"You didn't tell her to accept, did you?" Megan asked.

"Of course not, she's only eighteen."

"Then it's not your fault. Stop hitting yourself and tell me what happened."

He half smiled through his worry. And he did stop hitting himself. "Gina was purportedly staying with a friend this weekend. But the friend told her parents Gina and Scott have gone to Tennessee. To Gatlinburg."

"For a quickie wedding," Megan said. A bunch of towns up in the Smoky Mountains promoted themselves as wedding destinations, taking advantage of Tennessee's relaxed marriage laws, which allowed couples to get a license instantly and marry without a waiting period or blood test.

He nodded. "The friend's parents called my folks. Mom and Dad have tried Gina's cell phone, but she didn't pick up." He pulled out his own cell, and dialed his sister. "It's ringing." Then, a few seconds later, he said in disgust, "Voice mail."

Megan handed him her cell phone. "Try mine, she won't recognize the number."

But Gina didn't pick up that call either.

"Dad's asked me to go after them." Travis handed Megan's phone back. "Gatlinburg is two and a half, maybe three hours from here. Mom and Dad are getting on the road too, but it'll take longer from Jackson Creek." He thumped his fist into his other hand. "I'll kill her, my brainless, pain in the butt sister. As if Mom and Dad don't have enough on their minds."

"It's not all her fault. What about the other kid? Her boyfriend?"

"I'll kill him, too," Travis said irritably. "He's not a kid, he's twenty-four." He grabbed his jacket from the coat hook in the hallway, then came back into the dining room. "Can you carry on without me?"

She shoveled papers into a box. "I'm coming with you."

"No, you're not."

"I very much doubt Gina has decided to marry a twenty-four-year-old of her own free will."

He gaped. "You think he's *forcing* her?"

She wrapped her scarf around her neck. "I think he's making her prove her love. As you men seem to want to do."

"Don't compare me with some randy idiot," he said, outraged.

She hefted the box of papers into her arms. "I'm bringing this prenup with us. Five hours in the car are too good to waste."

"Fine. It'll help me stop thinking about killing Gina," he said grimly.

TRAVIS DROVE way faster than the law said he could, which meant they made it to the Smokies in just two and a half hours. It felt like less, because they spent most of the time talking about the Hoskinses.

Travis had kept in touch with his parents via cell phone as they drove. His mom and dad were an hour behind them on the road. His brothers were also on their way, traveling together.

But for now, responsibility for stopping Gina doing anything stupid rested with him.

He was glad Megan was along.

They passed the Welcome to Gatlinburg sign, a slab of timber with the words carved in an old-time font, toward ten-thirty.

It seemed every second shop in the town was either an outdoors store, a wedding chapel, a wedding dress rental store, or a photographer's studio. All were heavily decorated with Christmas themes.

Megan had called her paralegal, Trisha, on the way, and asked her to find out exactly how one went about getting married here. It turned out at this time of night, it wasn't easy—none of the independent wedding chapels were open after eight o'clock.

Trisha had spent a half hour phoning around the motels asking to be put through to Scott Taylor's room, until she hit pay dirt. Gina and her boyfriend were staying at Cupid's Inn Wedding Resort, a hotel with its own wedding chapel. Which probably meant they could get married any time they liked.

Which was worrying, but not as terrifying as the information vacuum they'd been in when they left Atlanta. He had Megan to thank for everything they knew—he was looking forward to telling his brothers that.

They found Cupid's Inn on the far side of town. The main building was a log-cabin-style structure, with a row of motel rooms stretching out either side.

Travis and Megan headed straight for the bar, where they used a house phone to call Scott's room. No reply. There was no sign of the young couple in the bar or the lobby. Megan volunteered to check the ladies' room, while Travis tried the men's.

"Maybe they went for a walk," Megan said doubtfully, as they reunited in the lobby.

"It's cold out," Travis said.

She grabbed his arm. "Travis, over there." She pointed to a sign that read Wedding Chapel. "Let's go look."

The chapel was in an annex that led off the lobby, part of the same building but tucked away. It was decorated in line with the log cabin theme: knotty pine everywhere, gingham curtains at the windows.

Near the entrance was a glass display case filled with wedding paraphernalia. Matching bride and groom baseball caps, long T-shirts printed with a wedding dress or a tuxedo, bridal veils, and bouquets of fake roses, lilies and baby's breath. Travis couldn't think of anything worse than celebrating a wedding with this kind of crap.

MEGAN DREW IN a breath when she spotted the young couple at the front of the chapel, heads together, engrossed in conversation. "Is that them?" she murmured to Travis.

He looked.

"Gina!" he snapped.

She jumped a mile high. Travis strode forward, pushing past Scott, and grabbed his sister by the hand. "You're not married already, are you?" He glanced around, as if he expected to find a minister skulking behind the lectern.

Gina tugged her hand free. "Butt out, Travis."

Megan stepped forward. "You're just checking out the chapel, right?"

Gina glowered, but said politely, "Right. We're getting married tomorrow morning, eight o'clock. Who are you?" She had the same dark hair as her brother and a face too dramatic to be called pretty, but which in about five years' time would be stunning.

"Megan's my lawyer," Travis said menacingly. Megan rolled her eyes.

"I'm a colleague. Megan Merritt." Megan shook Gina's hand. "This must be your fiancé."

"Scott," Gina said proudly.

"I won't let you do this," Travis said. "You've just started college, you have a lot of great years ahead."

"College isn't that big a deal." Gina grabbed one of the cushions from the front pew and clutched it to her chest. Megan wondered if she'd be hugging a stuffed animal at home. "I'm eighteen and I don't need anyone's permission to get married. I'd rather Mom and Dad approved, but it doesn't matter if they don't." Her voice quivered.

"Yeah," Scott said. A less-than-dynamic defense of his bride.

Travis eyed his sister as if he planned to throw her over his shoulder in a fireman's lift and march out. Megan put a hand on his arm. "You have more choices than that, Gina. Marriage and college aren't mutually exclusive."

"I hate being away from Scott. It's not enough, only getting down to Atlanta on weekends."

"You could switch to Georgia State."

"Duke is a great school," Travis objected.

"What's the point of staying in school if we both want to start a family?" Gina asked.

"A family! You do *not* get to throw away your life because some twenty-four-year-old pervert wants to get you pregnant," Travis growled. "You need to go to college and get a good job before you even think about having kids."

"You hypocrite!" Megan accused him. "You expect your wife to give up her career so she can stay home and look after your kids, but when your sister wants to do the same, you tell her she's wasting her life. So, what, it's just you who's so special a woman has to give up her own life for the honor of marrying you?"

A grin split Gina's face. "Yeah, Travis."

Travis's brows drew together. "I want you to have choices," he told his sister.

"Unlike your own wife, who'll have to do things your way," Megan interjected.

"This is nothing to do with you," he retorted.

"You're so right."

"I do have choices," Gina said. "I can choose to go to college or to get married. I choose marriage."

Megan charted a course between angering Travis further and pushing Gina into rebellion. "If you want marriage and kids, then you should have them."

"She should not!"

"But there's no hurry," Megan continued.

"I guess," Gina said. "But when Scott was a kid it was just him and his mom—he's really looking forward to us having a family of our own."

"Yeah," Scott managed to say again.

"That's a decision you need to be happy with, too," Megan said. "You already have enough people in your life who want you doing things their way—" she jerked a thumb at Travis "—you probably don't need another."

About to protest at Megan's undermining him, Travis finally clued in that she was making more headway with Gina than he was. Even if she'd had to label him a hypocrite to do it. And to be honest, it did sound as if Scott had pressured Gina into doing things his way.

He bit down on his desire to tell Gina exactly what he thought of her crackpot *fiancé* and said, "Megan's right."

Gina huffed. "Like you really believe that."

"Your family loves you and—" he almost choked on the words "—Scott loves you. Listen to what we have to say, but let your instinct guide you."

Gina loosened her grip on the cushion. "Really?"

No, not really. Really you need to get on a bus to Jackson Creek and let Dad at Scott with his shotgun. He nodded.

"*Do* you want to get married, Gina?" Megan asked. "In such a hurry?"

"Of course she does," Scott said.

Deliberately, Megan swiveled her gaze to him. He was a good-looking young guy, clean-cut, Travis noticed. If Gina was a few years older, her parents would probably think him the perfect match.

Megan's voice turned glacial in an exaggerated version of her courtroom manner. Features frozen in a disdainful glare, she said, "Excuse me, was I talking to you?"

Scott scooted backward, lips stretched in a nervous smile. "I love Gina. We've been dating nearly a year, it's just no one knew about it."

"That suggests you started dating when Gina was young enough for any intimacy to qualify as indecent assault, maybe even statutory rape," Megan said. "How much older than her are you?"

Go, Megan! Travis ran a hand over his mouth to conceal a smirk.

Scott paled. His mouth opened, then closed again.

"Getting married now is your choice," Megan said a whole lot more warmly to Gina. "But make sure it's a real choice. And if you choose to start a family, make that *your* choice, too. Your kids deserve nothing less than a hundred percent of your love. Otherwise you'll hurt them. Believe me, I know."

"Gina wouldn't hurt our kids," Scott protested. Once again, Megan quelled him with a glare, and he subsided into the front pew.

That gesture of resignation, of defeat, did as much as anything Megan could have said to shake Gina's confidence. Travis saw the flicker of doubt in her eyes.

"Gina, a great marriage is something to aspire to. I know I do," he said. "You can do a whole lot of things now that will build your character and your smarts and your creativity, so that by the time you eventually get married, you'll know how to build a strong, equal partnership."

He took Megan's hand. "Look at Megan." Her fingers fluttered in his. "She's the most amazing woman I know. She could have been snapped up years ago—" she quivered in indignation at being likened to some grocery store commodity, and he grinned "—but she's taking her time, making her choices. Refusing to settle for less than a guy's best offer."

Megan glared at him. "Gina, if you choose to get married now, Travis will respect that."

Uh-oh, he always felt that reverse psychology stuff was a big risk.

"But don't do anything now that will have you ending up like Travis, feeling as if you haven't fulfilled your potential."

Travis choked off a protest.

"Your brother has himself tied up in knots because he made the wrong choice for the right reasons," Megan said.

"Hey," Travis said. But Gina was lapping up the story of her brother's flawed approach to life, so he stifled his objections.

"If you decide to go ahead with the wedding, Travis will stand alongside you to give you in marriage to

Scott." It was a masterstroke. Megan had handed the decision back to Gina in a way that would give her the strength to make the right choice. Of course, if his sister chose to go ahead, he would have to do what Megan had committed him to. He hoped he could live with that. Hoped his parents could.

Gina's glance slid toward him, and he gave her an encouraging smile. She looked back at Megan and took a deep breath. "I want to marry Scott, but maybe not just yet."

"You said you love me," Scott protested. Megan gave Travis a blatant told-you-so look.

"We'll give you a ride home," she told Gina, as if they had mere blocks to travel, rather than nearly two hundred miles.

The back doors of the chapel burst open.

Megan whirled around to see two dark-haired men striding down the aisle. Their resemblance to Travis was unmistakable.

"Hey, guys, what took you so long?" Travis asked.

The leaner of the two brothers came charging at Gina much the way Travis had.

"Take it easy, Clay," Travis said. "Let me introduce you to the woman who convinced Gina it's better to wait a while for marriage." He tugged Megan forward. "Megan Merritt, Clay Jamieson."

Though Clay smiled in greeting, his face seemed strained. Bitterness lessened the impact of his good looks. He was the unhappily divorced one, Megan remembered as she shook his hand. He must have been worried sick about Gina making a mistake with a hasty marriage.

"And this is Brent," Travis said.

Brent was about her own age. But despite his resemblance to Travis, and despite the open appreciation in his eyes, she felt none of the electricity that surged between her and his older brother. Brent stood fractionally closer to her than courtesy dictated, and she knew she wasn't mistaken in her suspicion that he found her attractive.

"Sounds like we're in your debt," he said. "How can I thank you? Dinner? Maybe some dancing?"

"Back off," Travis warned.

"Whoa, just saying thank you to the lady." Brent held up both hands, but he was grinning with a mischief that Megan would bet had led to a few fistfights when they were kids.

She laughed, and found Travis's scowl directed at her.

"Mom and Dad were about ten minutes behind us," Clay said. "They should be here anytime now."

Gina shrieked. "Mom and Dad are coming?"

Scott paled, and he darted a glance at the door.

"What do you think they're going to do when their teenage daughter runs off to get married?" Travis demanded.

Gina bit her lip, so Megan said, "Travis will help you talk to your parents."

"Sure will." Travis put an arm around Gina's slender shoulders. She leaned into him.

The door opened at the back of the chapel; Hugh Jamieson walked in, a diminutive, dark-haired woman at his side.

"All under control, Dad," Travis called, as his father broke into a trot at the sight of Gina.

"Travis's *girlfriend* talked Gina out of it." Brent's emphasis was clearly a back-at-you to Travis for his overreaction; he grinned at Megan.

"Megan." Hugh did a double take, quickly masked, then introduced her to his wife, Ellie.

The older woman ignored the hand Megan extended. Instead, she stepped forward and planted a firm kiss on her cheek. "Thank you," she said. "For your help."

Briefly, Travis summarized for his parents what had transpired tonight. He gave Megan all the credit.

"I don't know about you all—" Hugh cracked his knuckles "—but I need a beer before we start for home. You can drive, Ellie."

Good grief, he sounded just like Travis, ordering the poor woman around. Imagine putting up with that for forty-odd years.

Ellie gave her husband a loving smile. "I'm afraid I'm in desperate need of a glass of wine, dearest. You'd better stick with coffee."

Hugh was all instant concern. "You okay, darlin'? This has been a big day."

"Nothing a nice Riesling won't fix." She took Clay's arm. "Take me to the bar."

Clay patted her hand. "Right this way, Mama."

In the bar, Hugh ordered white wine for Ellie and Megan, coffee for himself and Gina, and light beers for his sons. Megan found herself the center of attention, a place she never sought to be, except perhaps with her father. But it seemed Travis didn't often introduce women to his family, because the first question out of Ellie's mouth was, "Are you married?"

"I told you she's not, darlin'," Hugh said.

"Seeing anyone?" Ellie cocked her head to one side.

Beside her, Travis stiffened. Megan wanted to say yes. But when she'd kissed Travis back tonight, she'd known she could never feel anything for kind, nice Nick Stanton. "No," she said. "I'm not seeing anyone."

She glanced at Travis and caught a bright, hungry look in his eyes. *Don't bother,* she telegraphed. *I already turned down your best offer.*

"You're not at all what I expected." Ellie patted Megan's hand on the table, a motherly gesture that struck a chord in her memory. "Tell me about your family."

"Mom, don't hassle Megan," Travis said.

Ellie ignored him and squeezed Megan's fingers, a clear instruction to continue. Megan wondered what Ellie had been told about her, and by whom. She gave Travis's mom the condensed version of her family, but she must have waxed on a bit much about her father and her sisters, because Ellie said, "Your family is important to you. Good."

She clinked glasses with Megan, then pushed her glass away.

"Uh-oh, Mom's getting down to business," Brent scoffed.

"I hear you're a lawyer, Megan?"

Yikes, Brent was right. It was as if Megan passed an elimination round of questions and had made it to the semifinals of some contest whose rules she was pretty sure would not work in her favor. "That's right," she said.

"What else do you want from life?" Ellie asked, and Travis cringed in sympathy. "A pretty young thing like you must have more in mind than just work. Marriage…a family of your own."

Megan sent him a desperate look, and no wonder. His family wanted to know everything about her, short of her cup size. Actually, Brent looked as if he'd be pretty interested in her cup size.

Travis had studied her curves enough to be confident he knew.

"Megan's an amazing lawyer, Mom," he said. "She's totally dedicated to her career. Aren't you?"

"Well, yes." She didn't sound as if she appreciated him answering for her.

"I hear you don't want kids," Clay said.

Travis glared at his brother. All the while the word *compromise* ran through his head. Megan had used it.

"And I hear you're divorced with two kids and a lousy attitude," Megan said.

Brent snickered; Clay's color rose.

Ellie smacked him across the head. Lightly, to be sure, but with clear disapproval.

"Sorry," Clay muttered.

Travis rubbed his ear. Had his mom really just defended a woman who didn't want kids? Brent obviously liked Megan, too. And Gina. And she'd probably be good for Clay.

His mom was beaming at him, totally not subtle. He shook his head. He'd already hinted that he might love Megan, and she'd made it clear that what he was offering wasn't good enough.

Restlessness made him itch all over. He closed his eyes, tipped his head back and let the bar conversation flow around him. He needed to finish off the Hoskins divorce, then put this thing with Megan behind them. Then wait for Jonah's decision.

Only a few more days. By Christmas, it would all be over.

CHAPTER NINETEEN

ONE MORE DAY. That was all Megan had to survive. There might be meetings after today, though hopefully she could send Mark, her associate. But there would be no more of this intense, one-on-one interaction with Travis.

She yawned as she set her laptop bag down on Travis's dining table, remembering just in time to put a hand over her mouth.

"Thanks again for what you did last night," Travis said. They'd arrived back from Gatlinburg at two in the morning. Megan had set her alarm for five, and arrived at Travis's house before six to find him already working.

"We're going to nail this today, right?" she said. *Nail the divorce. Nail the end of our whatever-it-was we had.*

"You bet." He pulled a chair out for her.

Yesterday, they'd argued every point, haggled, harangued, and as a last resort negotiated. Today, the hours flew by in eerie calm as they agreed on one point after another. The prenup, a custody proposal, the works.

At six o'clock, they were done.

"That is the best damn divorce settlement I ever

saw." Megan straightened the edges of the document, still warm from Travis's laser printer.

"Modest *and* brilliant." Travis sobered. "Theo would be a fool not to make Merritt, Merritt & Finch his main law firm."

"Oh." She stared at him, wide-eyed.

"That's what this weekend was all about, remember?" he said. "Giving you the ammunition you need to convince your father."

"I'll ask Theo for his business tomorrow," she said. "But, Travis, you get as much credit for this as I do."

"I'll get it from my client," he said. "Each to their own."

She packed her copy of the settlement in her briefcase.

"I might visit Dad on the way home," she warned him. "Do some last-minute lobbying."

He nodded.

As always, he confused her. Did he want this job, or didn't he? "Are you planning on any last-minute schmoozing of my father?"

"That's not the way we tough guys do it," he said. "The manly way is to lay it out there, then we pretend we don't care if we get chosen or not."

She searched his face. "You care."

He nodded. "Don't tell your dad."

She smiled and shook her head. "Good luck, Travis."

"That's generous of you, Megs."

"The past two days you've made up for your despicable behavior," she said. "If anything will convince Theo to hire Merritt, Merritt & Finch, this document is it."

"Does that mean you forgive me?" he said, startled.

"I guess it does."

He swallowed. "Thank you."

He took her laptop out to the car and held the door open for her, waited until she'd buzzed down her window before he closed it. Megan adjusted her mirrors, which they didn't need, aware that this moment, right now, was the end of her association with Travis. Unless he showed up as her new boss. She fastened her seat belt. At last, she looked at him.

Travis appeared hazy...she realized there was moisture in her eyes. She glanced down, turned the key in the ignition. The engine purred to life.

"Goodbye," he said.

"Thanks for your help." She patted her briefcase on the seat beside her.

"Thanks for coming to Gatlinburg with me, too." Travis put his hands on the window opening, as if he could stop the car leaving.

"Glad to help. You have a wonderful family."

Travis realized they were both repeating nothings to delay her departure. "You know," he said on a moment's madness, "some women do combine career and family."

Her eyebrows rose.

"Or so I hear," he said.

A smile touched her lips. "That's progress, I guess." She put her hands on the steering wheel and looked straight ahead. "But I couldn't be one of those women, Travis. I wouldn't leave my kids with a nanny—kids need to know they're your priority. It would be a mistake to have them to please a husband whose career is just as demanding as mine." She took a deep breath. "So if the best offer still involves compulsory child-bearing as a prerequisite for your love..."

He let go of the car.

Megan released the hand brake. She was leaving. He wasn't going to stop her.

"Do you like 'Unchained Melody'?" he said suddenly.

"I hate that song!"

"Me, too," he said.

"Oh." It seemed to strike her how odd the question was. "Well…goodbye, Travis." Unconsciously, she tilted her face toward him.

He leaned in, kissed her on the lips. It wasn't much more than that first, accidental kiss at Salt. Once again, it burned him. This time it hurt.

She was miserable, too, he realized, her eyes downcast, her skin drawn with tension.

This is crazy, it's not happening. Stepping back took more strength than he could have imagined. "Goodbye, Megan."

It wasn't until she'd disappeared from view that he noticed the huge hole where his heart used to be.

"Oh, man," he groaned, and began jogging down the driveway. There was no sign of her car on the street. How stupid was he? How could he only just have figured out he loved Megan the way he'd always hoped to love a woman—the way his parents loved each other. A giving love, not just about him and what he wanted. A love that wanted her happiness above all else.

He loved her for her humor and her seriousness, her caution and her courage, her inner beauty and her outer sheer damned sexiness. *I love her.*

And he'd just let her go.

Oh, yeah, he'd nailed it all right.

TRAVIS PRESENTED the draft settlement to Barbara Hoskins on Monday morning. She loved it. In fact, she kissed him. Strictly platonically. Travis wondered if Theo would kiss Megan too, and tried not to worry about it. He asked his assistant to e-mail Megan's assistant with some minor alterations. Doubtless they'd receive similar amendments in return. But his staff could deal with that.

He sat down at his desk and called his parents. His mom answered the phone, so he had to listen to her going on about how great Megan was for ten minutes before he could insert a request to talk to his dad.

"Morning, son," Hugh said.

"Dad, there's something I need to tell you." He hurried on before his father could launch into a pro-Megan monologue. "It's not your responsibility to defend me. I don't want you arguing with your friends."

"I don't care what a bunch of old coots around here think about that firm of yours," Hugh retorted. "All I want is for you to be happy. That's what I get defensive about, son. The suggestion that you've worked so hard, but it didn't bring you what you want."

"Things are about to look up on that front," Travis said.

"Now you're talking," Hugh said. Then, innocently, "Your mother and I took a liking to that Megan."

"Me too, Dad. Me too."

Travis didn't bother replacing the handset in the receiver after he finished with his dad. He punched in Jonah Merritt's number.

"You were the last candidate I thought would try to butter me up at this late stage," the older man said.

"I'm calling to withdraw my application."

Silence.

"Whatever game you're playing, it won't force my hand," Jonah warned.

"No game," Travis said. "Sir, I appreciate you taking me seriously as a candidate, but I've realized the job won't give me what I want most."

"I thought you wanted the respect of your peers. If you don't think Merritt, Merritt & Finch will give you that—"

"It would, but what's more important is that I…" No, those words weren't for Jonah to hear. Not first, anyway. "Sir, have you decided who will get the job?"

"Almost." Jonah paused. "I have to admit you had me excited at the prospect of some of your changes."

Travis felt a pang for what he might be missing out on. He forged ahead. "Give the job to Megan."

"I beg your pardon?"

"She's the best lawyer I know, and you'll never find anyone more loyal to you and your vision for the firm," Travis said. "She might lack experience in some sectors, but there's no perfect candidate. Hell, if there was, I'd never have made it onto your list."

Jonah gave that Megan-like snort. "That's true."

Just like there was no perfect candidate for marriage, Travis thought. You had to go with the one you loved. He could only hope Megan would overlook his imperfections. He'd told her weeks ago that the woman he married would have a husband who always put her and their family ahead of his career. He'd come dangerously close to breaking that promise already. Never again.

"You're a smart man, by all accounts," Travis said to Jonah. "Be smart now."

After he ended the call, he felt strangely flat. He

knew what he had to say to Megan, knew what he wanted from her. But he had to give her a chance to hear Jonah's decision, whatever that would be. So she could make an informed choice, the way she'd told Gina to.

THEO WAS THRILLED with the settlement Megan proposed. Both the Hoskinses agreed to drop their contentious grounds for divorce, and after a couple of tweaks, agreed to by Barbara, they were done. On Tuesday, when Theo told her for the fourth time that she was brilliant, she asked him to give Merritt, Merritt & Finch a larger share of his business. He said yes, and immediately set in motion the transfer of a further twenty percent of his legal work. Enough to make him Merritt, Merritt & Finch's largest client.

Megan called her father with the good news. He sounded distracted, and it was impossible to tell what effect the news had on him.

What if twenty-five percent of Theo's business wasn't enough? What if she didn't get the job? And what if Travis did? They would be colleagues, in different divisions, but attending the same important meetings. Then one day he would find that woman who wanted to mother his children. He'd settle down, and as a senior partner Megan would be invited to his wedding, the christenings of his half-dozen children… Her mind ran rampant into a future filled with events celebrating Travis's happiness with some other woman.

Already, she felt sick to her stomach.

It was time to admit what she'd known, she realized now, from the moment Travis had stood up to her father on her behalf. She'd fallen in love with a chauvinistic, overprotective, bossy…sexy, charming, funny man who made her feel unique and cherished and special. With Travis.

"Hello, sweetheart." Her father stuck his head around her office door, startling her.

"Dad, hi, come in…" She was as distracted as she'd been that day she'd first seen Travis in The Jury Room, when she'd been waiting to hear her father's views on her application. She collected her thoughts, though with no real urgency.

Jonah closed the door behind him. Megan couldn't read his face. He would come in person whether it was good news or bad, she knew. If he had to hurt her, he would want to comfort her in his own inadequate way.

Jonah settled heavily in the chair in front of her desk. "I want you to take over the running of the firm."

The statement was so bald, so unembellished by emotion, it took a moment for Megan absorb it.

"You're giving me the job?" she squeaked.

Her father laughed. "Sure am. You deserve it, Megan, and there's no one I'd rather have in my seat than my own dear daughter."

"Dad…wow." She brushed away tears. "Thank you." She came around the desk to hug him. "I can't believe I actually made it."

He hugged her, patted her back, then released her. "You were up against some stiff competition, and you can be sure I wouldn't have given you the job if I didn't think you were the best of the lot."

"Have you told the others?" Travis would be so disappointed, her heart ached for him.

He shook his head. "I'll call them all this afternoon. Jamieson knows he's out, of course."

"Travis? Did you talk to him?"

Her father pursed his lips. "He pulled out yesterday—told me I'd be nuts not to hire you. I already knew that," he said severely, when her mouth opened in outrage. "That young man has a thing about speaking up where he's not wanted."

Travis had pulled out? Then told her dad to promote her? Megan's mind reeled. Of course, Jonah would never appoint her just because someone else told him to, but...why had Travis done it?

"Did he say why he was pulling out?"

"He said there's something he wants more." Disbelief resonated in Jonah's words. "I warned him, there's no other firm that can match Merritt, Merritt & Finch for credibility."

Megan started to smile. It couldn't be true...and yet she knew it, knew it like she knew her own name. *He wants me.* Travis's determination to help her win Theo's business, his pulling out of the job...it was because he loved her back.

The right kind of love, she was almost sure.

"Megan, are you all right?" Her father eyed her.

"Dad, maybe you should hold off on calling those other guys."

"What?" He put his hand to his chest, but it seemed more reflex than a real sign of ill health.

"There's something that might affect my ability to take the job."

"What do you mean?" he barked.

Her mind raced. "I hope it won't, but just in case, I can't risk...I mean, what if I need to make some kind of gesture, or..."

Jonah thumped the table, shutting her up. "I have

no idea what you're talking about. Megan, what are you saying?"

"I don't know. But I'll know soon. Just give me a little, a very little while." Megan stood and shepherded him to the door. She kissed his cheek. "Thanks, Dad, thanks so much."

He was still complaining when she closed the door on him.

She wanted to dance for joy, but first she had to think hard about how far she could go toward meeting Travis part of the way. How they could make this work. She asked her assistant to hold her calls.

"Mr. Jamieson called three times while your father was here," the girl said.

"I can't talk to him," Megan said. "Not yet."

She dithered far more than she'd expected. She knew what she wanted, she knew what he wanted, and the gap in between terrified her.

Slowly, she started to get her head around it. Let herself get used to the idea, without rushing. Just like she'd advised Gina. She forced herself to brave the department store madness and do her Christmas shopping. She chose a gift for Travis.

Several times that day, and the next, she heard her assistant say, "I'm sorry, Mr. Jamieson, Ms. Merritt is unavailable."

It wouldn't hurt him to hear that, she thought, given she was about to be the most shamelessly available woman he could imagine.

Thursday morning was Christmas Eve. Most people weren't working, but the office was open, and Megan had some loose ends to tie up. Besides, surely Travis would be sick of waiting and would find some creative way to butt into her life.

At ten o'clock, he appeared in the doorway. "Coffee delivery." He held up two take-out cups. "Latte for me, macchiato for you."

She got up and walked around her desk. "Macchiato? I've seen it on the menu, but I don't know exactly…"

"A single shot of espresso with a small amount of hot, foamed milk, just enough to stain the coffee."

"I love it already." She took the cup, sampled it. "Perfect, Travis. Just what I always wanted."

His dark eyes heated. She could have rushed into his arms right now, but she didn't.

"Thank you for pulling out of the job. Dad offered it to me."

"He would have anyway," Travis insisted. "You're the best person for it." He nudged her paper cup with his. "Congratulations."

"I told Dad I'd have to think about it."

His gaze sharpened. "Why?"

"That depends," she said, "on you."

She was standing very close to him now. She set her cup down on the desk; he did the same.

"Tell me more," he invited.

"I'm not exactly a great bet for a relationship, Travis," she said. "At least, not for a guy who wants to settle down and have kids."

Travis took her hands. "I love you, Megan. Will you marry me?"

Fireworks exploded inside her chest. "Wait," she said, "I haven't told you what a bad bargain you're getting."

"You forget," he said. "I know you."

He did. He had always seen her, known her, the way no one else did. Better, she could only hope, than she knew herself.

"I bought you a gift." She pulled the wrapped package out of her file cabinet. "Merry Christmas."

He flexed it experimentally. "It's a book. A mystery?"

"You could say that."

He tore the snowman-themed paper off. When he saw the gift, he stilled. "Megs." His voice choked.

"Name Your Baby."

He could barely speak.

"Travis, I can't promise just now to have your babies. I'm not saying I won't ever have them," she assured him. "I'm saying I need to be a different kind of person before I make that decision. The book's a promise that I'll try to be that person, that I want to be. But I don't know for sure if I can."

"You can," he said confidently, lifting first one of her hands to his mouth for a kiss, then the other. "You can be anything you want. I love you, Megan. Will you marry me?" He grinned. "Is it time to say that now?"

"Not yet." She planted a kiss on his chin, as a down payment. "About my new job. I want it, but if it means you and I aren't going to work, then, well, I can stick with what I'm doing now."

"I want you to have the job," he said. "I love you, Megs. Will you marry me?"

"I love your family," she said. "I want to be a part of it."

He kissed the tip of her nose. "Answer the damn question."

"I love you, Travis. I will marry you."

Joy swept over his face. "You have no idea how good it feels to hear that." He folded her into his embrace and kissed her passionately, walking her backward so she could perch on the edge of her desk. His fingers combed her hair, pulling it from its loose knot so it fell around her shoulders.

Megan gloried in the taste of him, in the tenderness of his touch, in his unspoken but crystal-clear promise of forever.

When they surfaced, she was shaking.

"I got you a gift, too," he said. The shape of the little package was a dead giveaway.

Megan tore the paper off and opened the crimson velvet box. The ring was magnificent. A princess-cut topaz, surrounded by diamonds. "I love it," she said.

"It matches your eyes." Travis slid it onto her finger. "There." He gazed at the ring, a proprietary gleam in his eyes. "*Now* we've nailed it."

"There's just one more thing," Megan said. "I hope it's not going to be a deal breaker."

"I won't let it be." But visibly, he braced himself. "Go on."

"Absolutely, definitely, no prenup allowed," she said.

Travis whooped and punched the air. "Megs, my darling, you just got yourself a husband."

EPILOGUE

"THANK YOU for your time, ladies and gentlemen, that concludes our meeting." Megan closed the folder in front of her and smiled around the boardroom table, ending with her husband at the far end.

The atmosphere relaxed immediately, and Merritt, Merritt & Jamieson's partners broke into less formal discussions in twos and threes.

"One thing my co-managing partner forgot to mention…" Travis's voice, full of laughter, brought them back to attention.

The sound of a loud gurgle was followed by a belch. All eyes turned to Megan. "Excuse me," she said, and pushed her chair back so she could look beneath the table. "What do you want, little one?"

Her six-month-old daughter blinked in her infant seat, still waking up from the nap that had mercifully lasted the length of the meeting. That was the problem with part-time babysitters—occasionally, when she and Travis were both required to attend a meeting, Megan had to bring Sophia into the office.

"I forgot to say, Travis and I will be on vacation next week," she announced. "It's our third wedding anniversary. You can reach us on our cells in an emergency, but otherwise, we'll see you in a week."

The team filed out in a cloud of congratulatory murmurs. At last only Travis, Megan and baby Sophia, her seat now elevated to the boardroom table, remained.

Travis took Megan in his arms. "Did the sitter not show up, or are you already grooming our daughter to take over the firm?"

She grinned. "She just missed her daddy. I should never have agreed to job-share with you. You're much better with Sophia, she loves her days at home with you."

He laughed, and Sophia gurgled in delight. "You fight me tooth and nail every time I get near her," Travis teased Megan.

She shrugged. "That's just maternal instinct. Even the most unlikely women have it."

He snared her with an arm about her waist, pulled her to him and took her mouth with a kiss that left her breathless. "You, my darling, are not unlikely. You're an exceptionally loving and giving person."

She kissed him again. "I love *you*, that's for sure."

"And you always will," he said with satisfaction.

Megan chuckled against his chest.

"What's so funny?"

"I can't afford to give up on this marriage," she said. "I figure it's going to take another fifty years to knock those chauvinist tendencies out of you."

He kissed her long and hard. "Bring it on, Megs. I'm all yours."

* * * * *

Don't miss Cynthia's story—the last of
THOSE MERRITT GIRLS—*by Abby Gaines,*
when HER SURPRISE HERO hits the shelves
in January 2010!

*Celebrate 60 years of pure
reading pleasure with Harlequin®!
Just in time for the holidays,
Silhouette Special Edition® is proud to present*
New York Times *bestselling author
Kathleen Eagle's*
ONE COWBOY, ONE CHRISTMAS

Rodeo rider Zach Beaudry was a travelin' man—
until he broke down in middle-of-nowhere South
Dakota during a deep freeze. That's when an
angel came to his rescue....

"Don't die on me. Come on, Zel. You know how much I love you, girl. You're all I've got. Don't do this to me here. Not *now*."

But Zelda had quit on him, and Zach Beaudry had no one to blame but himself. He'd taken his sweet time hitting the road, and then miscalculated a shortcut. For all he knew he was a hundred miles from gas. But even if they were sitting next to a pump, the ten dollars he had in his pocket wouldn't get him out of South Dakota, which was not where he wanted to be right now. Not even his beloved pickup truck, Zelda, could get him much of anywhere on fumes. He was sitting out in the cold in the middle of nowhere. And getting colder.

He shifted the pickup into Neutral and pulled hard on the steering wheel, using the downhill slope to get her off the blacktop and into the roadside grass, where she shuddered to a standstill. He stroked the padded dash. "You'll be safe here."

But Zach would not. It was getting dark, and it was already too damn cold for his cowboy ass. Zach's battered body was a barometer, and he was feeling South Dakota, big time. He'd have given his right arm to be climbing into a hotel hot tub instead of a brutal blast of north wind. The right was his free arm anyway.

Damn thing had lost altitude, touched some part of the bull and caused him a scoreless ride last time out.

It wasn't scoring him a ride this night, either. A carload of teenagers whizzed by, topping off the insult by laying on the horn as they passed him. It was at least twenty minutes before another vehicle came along. He stepped out and waved both arms this time, damn near getting himself killed. Whatever happened to *do unto others?* In places like this, decent people didn't leave each other stranded in the cold.

His face was feeling stiff, and he figured he'd better start walking before his toes went numb. He struck out for a distant yard light, the only sign of human habitation in sight. He couldn't tell how distant, but he knew he'd be hurting by the time he got there, and he was counting on some kindly old man to be answering the door. No shame among the lame.

It wasn't like Zach was fresh off the operating table—it had been a few months since his last round of repairs—but he hadn't given himself enough time. He'd lopped a couple of weeks off the near end of the doc's estimated recovery time, rigged up a brace, done some heavy-duty taping and climbed onto another bull. Hung in there for five seconds—four seconds past feeling the pop in his hip and three seconds short of the buzzer.

He could still feel the pain shooting down his leg with every step. Only this time he had to pick the damn thing up, swing it forward and drop it down again on his own.

Pride be damned, he just hoped *somebody* would be answering the door at the end of the road. The light in the front window was a good sign.

The four steps to the covered porch might as well have been four hundred, and he was looking to climb them with a lead weight chained to his left leg. His eyes were just as screwed up as his hip. Big black spots danced around with tiny red flashers, and he couldn't tell what was real and what wasn't. He stumbled over some shrubbery, steadied himself on the porch railing and peered between vertical slats.

There in the front window stood a spruce tree with a silver star affixed to the top. Zach was pretty sure the red sparks were all in his head, but the white lights twinkling by the hundreds throughout the huge tree, those were real. He wasn't too sure about the woman hanging the shiny balls. Most of her hair was caught up on her head and fastened in a curly clump, but the light captured by the escaped bits crowned her with a golden halo. Her face was a soft shadow, her body a willowy silhouette beneath a long white gown. If this was where the mind ran off to when cold started shutting down the rest of the body, then Zach's final worldly thought was, *This ain't such a bad way to go.*

If she would just turn to the window, he could die looking into the eyes of a Christmas angel.

* * * * *

*Could this woman from Zach's past
get the lonesome cowboy to come in
from the cold...for good?
Look for
ONE COWBOY, ONE CHRISTMAS
by Kathleen Eagle
Available December 2009
from Silhouette Special Edition®*

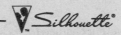

Silhouette®

SPECIAL EDITION

**FROM *NEW YORK TIMES* AND *USA TODAY*
BESTSELLING AUTHOR**

KATHLEEN EAGLE

ONE COWBOY,
One Christmas

When bull rider Zach Beaudry appeared
out of thin air on Ann Drexler's ranch,
she thought she was seeing a ghost of
Christmas past. And though Zach had
no memory of their night of passion years
ago, they were about to share a future
he would never forget.

*Available December 2009
wherever books are sold.*

SSE65493

Visit Silhouette Books at www.eHarlequin.com

HARLEQUIN®

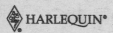

INTRIGUE®

FIRST NIGHT

BY

DEBRA WEBB

COLBY AGENCY

To prove his innocence, talented artist Brandon Thomas is in a race against time. Caught up in a murder investigation, he enlists Colby agent Merrilee Walters to help catch the true killer. If they can survive the first night, their growing attraction may have a chance, as well.

Available in December wherever books are sold.

www.eHarlequin.com

HI69440